gadget girl

gadget
girl

The Art of Being Invisible

SUZANNE KAMATA

GEMMA

BOSTON

First published by GemmaMedia in 2013.

GemmaMedia
230 Commercial Street
Boston, MA 02109 USA

www.gemmamedia.com

Printed in the United States of America

17 16 15 14 13 1 2 3 4 5

978-1-936846-38-2

Library of Congress Cataloging-in-Publication Data

Kamata, Suzanne, 1965–
    Gadget Girl : the art of being invisible / Suzanne Kamata.
        pages cm
    "Gadget Girl began as a novella published in Cicada. The
story won the SCBWI Magazine Merit Award in Fiction and was
included in an anthology of the best stories published in Cicada
over the past ten years"—Provided by publisher.
    Summary: Aiko Cassidy, a fourteen-year-old with cerebral
palsy, tired of posing for the sculptures that have made her mother
famous, dreams of going to Japan to meet her father and become a
great manga artist, but takes a life-changing trip to Paris, instead.
    ISBN 978-1-936846-38-2 (pbk.)
    [1. Coming of age—Fiction.   2. Artists—Fiction.   3. Mothers
and daughters—Fiction.   4. Single-parent families—Fiction.
5. Cerebral palsy—Fiction.   6. Comic books, strips, etc.—
Fiction.   7. Paris (France)—Fiction.   8. France—Fiction.]
I. Title.
    PZ7.K12668Gad 2013
    [Fic]—dc23

                                                        2012051566

Cover design: Night & Day Design

For Lilia

contents

PART ONE

michigan

"Who are you and what are you doing with that
electric toothbrush?"

—Chaz Whittaker to Lisa Cook
Gadget Girl, "Attack of the Zombie Ninjas"

1

My father has blue hands. Or at least that's what Mom tells me—one of the few facts I've been able to wring out of her. See, he's the eldest son of one of the last indigo producers in his village on the Japanese island of Shikoku. His family has been growing indigo for generations—centuries, even—since back in the time of the shoguns.

"You were named after that plant," Mom told me. "*Ai* means indigo. *Ko* means child."

Indigo is my destiny.

The color blue begins with a seed planted in early spring. After the first green sprigs pop through the earth, the seedlings are transplanted to fields. The leaves are still green then. Later, in the hot, sticky days of summer, the plants are harvested and dried out. Then the leaves are tossed into a vat with wood ash, lye, and wheat bran and fermented.

"It's very stinky," Mom told me, "but it produces the most beautiful hue—the color of a storm-bruised sky."

The first time she explained all this, she took a deep blue cloth from a drawer and unfurled it over my lap. "This is for you," she said. "Your father dyed this."

I traced the blue circles with my fingers and brought the cloth to my nose. When I inhaled, I caught that earthy, vegetable scent. "I want to do this," I said. I was young then, maybe six or seven years old. I imagined dunking all of my clothes into a vat of indigo and turning them blue.

"Then your hands will look as if they were smeared with blueberries," she said, laughing.

My father's hands were tinged from dipping cloth into the dye. No matter how many times he washed them, she said, they were always a little bit blue.

"It takes a long time to master the art of dyeing," she said. "And it's very hard work to grow and harvest the indigo plants."

Mom told me about the dawn-to-dusk labor and the crouching in the fields. Being a farmer's wife was hard work. She would hardly have had any time for her art. I wondered sometimes if that's why she hadn't married my father.

There's a small terra-cotta pot filled with dirt on my windowsill. I'm trying to grow indigo. Michigan is not the best place for it, however. Indigo plants like heat and humidity. They grow well in tropical climates or steamy greenhouses. Back in the antebellum era, it was a major crop in sultry, mosquito-infested South Carolina. Indigo also does well in India and, of course, in Shikoku. I've been trying to give my pot lots of sunlight, but this room is the coolest, temperature-wise, in the house.

Maybe Mom didn't want to slave away as a farm wife, but I figure if I can manage to grow an indigo plant in my bedroom in the chilly-in-spring state of Michigan, my father would be more than happy to take me on. The only problem is that my gardening skills suck. It could be that I have a black thumb. I've never tried to grow anything else, it's true, and so I should have no reason to believe that I can get a plant to thrive, but I can't bring myself to give up. I buy the seeds via the Internet. I've tried sprouting them out-side in late spring and a couple of times in summer. This is my second attempt with a pot. One day I'll get it right.

I take a long look at the pot, but there is no hint of green, no long-awaited sprout. I rotate the pot any-way, and spritz the dirt with water.

I sigh and move on to my other project. I reach under my mattress for my sketchbook and get to work on the next installment of *Gadget Girl*, my secretly self-published manga.

Lisa Cook is a klutz, but her alter ego, Gadget Girl, is perfect in every way. Actually, she's beyond perfect. After gulping down a shooting star, she was endowed with superhuman strength and extreme precision. What I mean by that is, she can thread a needle on the first try. She can put on mascara with one whisk of the wand, without having to wipe away stray black clumps. She can tie her shoes in seconds. In other words, she's everything that I'm not.

I have cerebral palsy, which messes up my motor skills. My right arm and hand are fully functional. I can write and draw, use chopsticks and other utensils skillfully, and even do up buttons. But my left hand? Forget about it. My fingers are stiff, and curl inward, and sometimes my arm develops a life of its own, thrashing anyone within reach. The CP affects my left leg, too. I can't completely feel what's going on down there. It's as if my circulation has been cut off and my leg has gone to sleep. But I can get around okay, even though I limp.

Gadget Girl, however, can put just the right spin on a Swiss Army knife, hurl it, and open a bottle of pop from fifty feet away. Or she can use an eggbeater to start up a maelstrom and blind an opponent with flying dust. She's good with her hands. In every episode, she has to rescue a dude-in-distress. This guy is usually Chaz Whittaker, an all-around athlete who looks a lot like Chad Renquist, this guy in my class. Lisa/ Gadget Girl is secretly in love with Chaz, but one kiss from a normal boy and she'll be zapped of her superpowers forever, so she keeps her feelings to herself.

Better to save the planet than to give in to love. Sacrifices must be made.

She lives with her guardian, Hiro Tanaka, the only person who knows her true identity. Tanaka is a brilliant, reclusive botanist. He's developing plants that can cure diseases even better than stem cells can. He's super famous, but Gadget Girl is protecting his privacy.

I'm working on volume two, number three. I've got the panels sketched out in blue pencil (which doesn't show up when it's photocopied), and now all I've got to do is finish inking and lettering with my black calligraphy pen. In this story, Gadget Girl goes to the Blue Ridge Mountains for a bit of rest and relaxation. In the previous issue, she welcomed a group of visiting aliens at a resort in the Southwest. She was in the process of making a soufflé for the guests when Chaz got into trouble. He was in the desert on a group tour. He got separated from his buddies when he went off to take a picture of a cactus. Suddenly, he was attacked by a band of marauding jackrabbits. Gadget Girl, who has a sixth sense when it comes to Chaz, rushed from the kitchen, whisk in hand, and whipped up a sandstorm to drive away the long-eared demons. Once again safely on the tour bus, Chaz sighed and said, "My heroine!"

I'm just about finished when I hear my mother call out my name. "Come here!" she shouts. "I need your help."

2

I'm standing in my mother's studio, feet turned out, one hand on my hip, the other curled at my waist.

"That's perfect, Aiko," Mom says. She tucks a strand of blonde hair back into her scrunchie, then takes up her chisel again. "Do you think you can hold that pose for about three more minutes?"

"Yeah," I say. But when she's not looking, I move my right foot—my good foot—a few inches just to mess with her.

I'm surrounded by sculptures and sketches and paintings of myself at every age. There's me with long brown hair, me with short hair. Me, with my high forehead and full lips, everywhere I look. When I was little, I couldn't flex my feet very well. I was always on my tippy toes, which inspired Mom to sculpt me as a ballerina. *Aiko, En Pointe*, the sculpture that got Mom a write-up in the *New York Times*, stands straight across from me. I imagine her, my three-year-old self in stone, winking. I wink back. *I know you don't want to stand here like this, kid. Don't worry. It'll be over soon.*

"Okay, great." Mom smiles and brushes some dust off her jeans. "You can go now."

My stomach lets out a loud growl. We both glance at the clock on the wall. It's already six.

"What's for dinner?" It's her turn to cook.

"Oh, honey," she says. "I guess we'll just order a pizza."

I roll my eyes. Not again. We just had frozen pizza two nights ago. From what I've read and seen in movies, no self-respecting Japanese mother would ever make her kid order pizza. On the Internet, I've seen pictures of lunch boxes made by Japanese moms— rice balls shaped like Hello Kitty, wieners carved into crabs, carrots cut like flowers. My mother can barely manage the microwave. Could that be another reason why my father didn't marry her?

"I'll make the call," I say.

"You do that. My wallet is on the kitchen counter. There should be enough money in there for a large."

I turn away.

"I'm going to enter this one in the Tokyo International Art Concours," Mom says, her voice pulling me back.

My ears perk up. "Tokyo?"

"It's a big prize." She rubs her fingers together.

Money. Lots of it. "First prize would be like winning the jackpot."

One thing I've learned as the daughter of an artist is that "rich" and "famous" do not necessarily go hand in hand. Although Mom's sculptures sell for thousands of dollars, not everyone has that kind of money to throw around. It's been a while since she's made a sale. A big prize could mean a better class of pizza. New clothes. Or, best of all, winning this prize might mean a trip to Japan.

Even so, this is the first sculpture she's done of me since I've started wearing a bra, and it seems different somehow. It's not a nude or anything, but the thought of the judges, *strangers*, running their eyes and maybe their hands over those lumps on the chest kind of creeps me out.

"Well," I say, "Good luck with that."

I go back into the house and pick up the phone. We order pizza so often that I've memorized the number. The menu, too. I order a large pepperoni with extra cheese and open up Mom's faux crocodile wallet to take out some dollar bills.

I notice a photo tucked behind her credit card and pull it out. It's a boy, about thirteen years old. His hair is shaved close to his head and he has glasses. He looks Japanese. There's something familiar about him. Could it be a snapshot of my dad as a child? No, it can't be. This print looks new. It must have been taken recently. I look on the back, but there's no writing there. Hmm. Well, maybe it's a photo of some kid she met on a school visit, someone she wanted to sketch.

Mom's studio door squeaks open, so I quickly put the photo back.

We set the table with paper plates and plastic cups and sit down to wait for our dinner to arrive.

Mom yanks off her scrunchie and shakes out her hair. "Guess who I got a call from today?"

I shrug. "Grandma?"

"Try again."

"Rolfe?" Rolfe, a foreign correspondent, is her ex-boyfriend. We haven't heard from him in a while, not since she dumped him and started going out with Raoul, whom I have yet to meet.

"Wrong." She sighs. Obviously I'm not trying hard enough. "It was Mr. Hodge."

My eighth grade art teacher? Why would he be calling her? Am I not mixing my colors correctly?

"He invited me to come for a school visit!"

Oh. No. "You turned him down, right?"

"Why would I do that?"

"Maybe because it would embarrass me?" I say.

Mom has a job teaching art at a community college in Grand Rapids. But she makes a big point of visiting schools to talk about her "mission."

"Other parents have been called in for Career Day, haven't they? Besides, everything's all set up for next Friday," she says.

Before I can say another word, the doorbell rings. It's the pizza guy, but suddenly I've lost my appetite.

3

When dinner's over and the paper plates have been wadded up and stuffed into the trash, Mom goes back to her studio and I go to my room.

I love my bedroom. I've got this holiday-in-Japan thing going on with my decor. If I can't live in the country, at least I can pretend. My bed is covered with a quilt made of recycled kimonos that I found at a flea market—squares of brocade with cranes and chrysanthemums. And I keep my bracelets and stuff in a lacquer bowl. On the wall I've got posters of my favorite manga characters, scenes from anime, and a photo of Young Mom on a Japanese side street, dressed up in a *yukata* and *geta*, those wooden sandals that go clunkety-clunk when you walk on concrete. My desk is a low table, the kind that Japanese writers kneel at as they scribble their famous works. Only I use mine mostly for homework and drawing, not for writing novels or poetry.

I sit down at the table to call my best friend, Whitney.

We've been tight ever since the day in fourth grade when we both showed up at school in the same Sailor Moon T-shirt. No one else in our class had any idea who she was. Japanese manga wasn't exactly huge in our dinky Michigan town. But Whitney, she knew all about Sailor Moon, plus she had the entire collection of comics. During recess, Whitney played Venus Moon to my Sailor Moon, or sometimes the other way around, and everyone else thought we were weird. I guess they still think that, but they pretty much leave us alone. Whitney is maybe the only girl on earth who understands me.

So her response to my big news is a little strange.

"Your mom is cool," she says. "Everyone will love her."

Where's the sympathy in that?

"If she comes into my classroom, I'm leaving," I say. I picture myself dragging my leg along the empty hallway, or sitting on the lawn outside, all alone.

"Oh, please. Your mom should share her art, and so should you."

Share *my* art, she means. Whitney is the biggest fan of *Gadget Girl*.

"Speaking of which," Whitney continues, "Nathan finished making copies of the latest issue. I'll give them to you at school tomorrow."

"Thanks."

Whitney's older brother, Nathan, works part-time

at Kinko's. I give him money from my allowance for printing and stapling, and he takes the stacks of comics to the indie book store, the music store, and the anarchist café downtown. He sets out a coffee can at each place for donations, and usually there are a few coins rattling around inside at the end of the week. Whitney and Nathan are the only people who know that I'm the artist.

I don't draw for fame. I don't do it for the money, either. I'm in training now, until I can apprentice myself to one of my heroes. That's another big reason why I want to go to Japan—all of my favorite manga artists are there, and I want to believe that at least one of them would be willing to take me in and help me improve. Or at least let me make tea and clean up ink stains while I look over her shoulder.

4

Just before the start of Wednesday's English class, I meet up with Whitney in front of my locker. Today she's wearing a short-sleeved white blouse with pleats and a black pencil skirt.

"Wanna try?" she asks, striking a pose.

"Hmm." I take in the cross dangling from her neck. "Madonna in *Desperately Seeking Susan*?"

She rolls her eyes. I can never get it right.

"Not quite, honey. Susan Sarandon in *Dead Man Walking*. The nun?"

"Oh. Yeah."

Whitney still wears manga T-shirts once in a while, but her look is mostly borrowed from movie stills these days. Today's outfit is pretty tame, but when she's obsessing on a period piece, say, *Shakespeare in Love*, she'll come to school in more of a costume.

Guessing game over, she hands me the latest edition of *Gadget Girl*. The photocopies are tucked into a manila envelope so that no one else can see.

"Yay!" I peek inside. "Thanks a lot!"

She reaches for the pages, but I shake my head. "Not here."

I motion to Madison Fox and her posse, grooming at the back of the room. They've whipped out their compacts and lip gloss. They're not paying any attention to us, but still. I don't want to risk exposure.

Whitney sighs. "You should just go ahead and tell people," she says. "You've got a fan base now. They would support you."

"No," I say. What if they just felt sorry for me? What if they saw *Gadget Girl* as an expression of my fantasies? Wouldn't it make them pity me more? But I don't say any of this to Whitney, even if she is my best friend. I pretend that it's all about the mystique I'm creating, and letting my art speak for itself.

"I don't get my allowance till next week," I say. "You think Nathan would print out the rest of the copies anyway? Put it on my tab?"

Whitney shrugs. "I can float you a loan. My dad just sent a big check. Any new distribution points?"

"The usual will be fine, I guess—bowling alley, arcade, anarchist coffee house." Plus, I'll send some copies out to my zinester friends. I've got some extra envelopes, so I'll prepare them for mailing during study hall. Mom is taking me to the post office after school.

When the last bell rings, I find Mom's car in the queue in front of the building.

"Hi there," she says, as I crawl into the back seat.

There's a manila envelope on the passenger seat beside her. She sees me noticing it. "I've got something of my own to put in the mail," she says. "This is my entry for the Tokyo International Art Concours."

Oh, right. *Aiko, in Fourth Position*. Of course, she's not sending the sculpture itself—just photos for now.

It would be cool if she won—it would be great! But I'm not getting my hopes up. I remember that she entered last year, too. And the year before that. She sends off entries to art competitions all over the world—Prague, Paris, Taiwan—but so far her successes have been purely domestic. Her last show was in North Carolina.

Luckily, there's not much of a line at the post office. I go up to the window first. Mom is right behind me, but she doesn't ask me what's in the envelopes, which is cool. Sometimes she actually seems to understand my need for privacy.

I hand over some money to the postal clerk and watch her stamp the envelopes and put them on a pile.

I stand there blinking for a moment, imagining my superheroine travelling all over the country. "Thanks." I step out of the way.

Mom is humming as we go back to the car. "I want to celebrate finishing the sculpture," she says. "And I want to thank you for being my model. How about I take you shopping?"

"Yeah, sure." To tell the truth, shopping's not my favorite thing. It takes forever for me to try on clothes, and then there are the crowds and the little kids staring. But Mom isn't always so free and easy with her credit card. I need to take advantage of this opportunity.

The clothing district is down by the riverfront, near the building which once housed the Grand Theater. Now it's a restaurant with a marquee, but at one time it was like a ballroom, with a chandelier hanging from the ceiling. Whitney would have loved watching movies there.

A few doors down, there's a café owned by former hippies who sell cups of organic coffee and desserts made with carob. They also host local acoustic musicians and travelling folk singers.

Mom and I hit up one of the more expensive clothing boutiques. The mannequins in the window are in turquoise sequins and pink taffeta and daring strapless knee-high black dresses. It's prom season. Some girls from my class will probably be shopping here for the end-of-the-year middle school dance, but not me. When I see those dresses—all that tulle and sparkle—I want to run (ha!) back to the car and bury my head in the seat cushions.

Normally, I'm partial to dark colors. Black. Midnight blue. I read about Japanese Bunraku puppeteers who wear black clothes and hoods while maneuvering three-foot-high puppets across the stage. Because they're in black, the audience doesn't really notice them. Wearing black is like being in the dark. It makes you hard to see. Almost invisible.

Unfortunately, there seems to be nothing black or indigo or even grey in this store. I spy a rack of swirly patchwork skirts and make my way toward them. I take a skirt off the rack and hold it up to my waist. It's white, but appliquéd with bright red and yellow flowers. It's totally Salma Hayek in *Frida*! Frida Kahlo was this Jewish-Mexican painter whose leg was shrunken from polio. (As part of Mom's campaign to Help Aiko Feel Good About Herself, I have been introduced to any number of potential mixed-race role models.) Frida wore bright skirts to cover her bad leg, or maybe to distract from her disability. Maybe this skirt could do the same for me. I find a couple more that I like and show them to Mom.

"Those are pretty," she agrees, and takes them to the counter. It's too much of a drama to try them on here in the store. We'll take these home and if they don't fit, Mom will bring them back.

If we're very, very lucky, I'll be able to put them in my suitcase and wear them in Japan.

5

Friday, sixth period. I'm sitting at my table, waiting for art to begin. Normally this would be my favorite class, but today I just want it to be over with. My stomach is going through the spin cycle, and my left arm is jerking, like it does when I get nervous.

Within the next five minutes, Mom will walk through the door. I'm hoping that she won't embarrass me. Better yet, she'll totally ignore me and I can pretend that I'm invisible. I look away from the door, trying to distract myself.

Mr. Hodge, the art teacher, has taped our last assignment—tissue paper collages in shades of blue—all over the walls. Kind of a lame project, if you ask me, though Madison Fox managed to make hers look like a hydrangea. I pasted my blue tissue paper squares in the shape of handprints and called the collage "My Father's Hands." Although Mr. Hodge frowned when I told him the title, I got an A. But truly, tissue paper is not my medium. I'm a pen-and-ink kind of girl.

The bell rings, and in stumbles Chad Renquist, male model and class heartthrob. His last big gig was modeling running gear for the catalog of a sporting goods store in Grand Rapids. He's not the kind of guy you'd figure would choose art as an elective, but then again, his work is pretty good. Maybe he's a closet Picasso. His collage is a fairly convincing self-portrait: "Blue Chad."

Since I'm not part of Chad's world, I can pretty much stare at him whenever I want to. His hair is clipped neatly around his ears now, and he's got broad shoulders and chocolate eyes. On a warm day like today, when he's wearing short sleeves, you can see his biceps, hard as apples, and the veins popping out on his forearms. He obviously lifts weights. He also obviously has a girlfriend—head cheerleader Madison Fox.

Chad goes over to talk to Madison for a moment. She's another of the Beautiful Ones. They laugh about something, then Chad goes back to the table where he usually sits, far away from me, and drops into his chair just as the teacher arrives.

Mr. Hodge likes to make an entrance. He goes off to the faculty lounge between classes and changes his smock or whatever, then waits till we're all seated before he bursts through the door. He comes in today with a magazine in one hand and slowly surveys the room.

"Good afternoon, my minions," he booms. "Today, as you may recall, we have a special guest."

I sink down in my seat. My left arm starts to spaz a little, so I grab onto it with my right hand.

"Laina Cassidy, whom most of you know is Aiko's mother, has agreed to come in today and talk to us about sculpting." At this point, he opens the magazine, which just hit the newsstands days ago, and holds it up to show us Mom, posing in her studio. She's wearing an evening gown and clutching a chisel. Her face is buried under gobs of makeup and her hair is messy, but perfect. It's so staged.

"That's *Aiko's* mom?" Jason Tran blurts out. His family moved here last fall from Muskegon. He's probably the only one in this class who's never seen my mother. He looks from the magazine to me and back again, his mouth hanging open in surprise.

I get that a lot. Strangers often assume I'm adopted because we look nothing alike. My eyes and hair are dark, and my forehead is sort of broad. Also, I've got short, thick eyebrows which I definitely didn't inherit from the Cassidy side of the family.

Suddenly everybody's looking at me. I grab my arm tighter and will myself to disappear. *Mr. Hodge, get control of your class.*

He must mind-read because he loudly clears his throat, drawing everyone's attention away from me. "Laina is very, very busy," he says, "so we're lucky that she was willing to take time out of her schedule to share with us today."

I smirk. Believe me, it doesn't take much to get "Laina" into a classroom. And I'm guessing that Mr. Hodge's reasons for inviting her to speak to our class are beyond just exposing us to educational opportunities.

"Well, then," he says, straightening the lapels of his white lab coat. "Without further ado, I give you the brilliant Laina Cassidy."

I take a deep breath as the door opens and she walks in.

Laina—Mom—is carrying a big cardboard box. Mr. Hodge hurries over to relieve her of her burden. While he's setting it on the table, her eyes dart around until she finds me. She gives me a little smile and then looks away. I've made her promise not to single me out. I'm pretty sure she won't yank me to the front of the class to use as a volunteer. I let go of my arm. The spasms have stopped. Everyone is looking at my mother now. No one is paying any attention to me. Just the way I like it.

"A lot of people think that sculptors take a chunk of rock and just start chipping away," Mom begins, "but nothing could be further from the truth."

She takes out a pad of paper and a pencil and starts sketching the student in front of her, who just happens to be Chad.

"I start with a drawing of my subject," she says. "Sometimes I draw from life, other times from photographs. And sometimes, I just use my imagination."

She is silent for a few minutes, her pencil busily scratching away, and then she stops and shows us what she's done.

"Oooh," the class says. In just a few minutes, she has captured the essence of Chad—the high cheekbones, the slight smirk, the dimpled chin. Everyone thinks she is amazing.

I understand that my mother is extremely talented. She can, as one critic wrote, make a rock look soft. Her sculptures are full of curves, rounded knees and elbows and soft bellies. I'm proud of what she does, but at the same time I wish that her art didn't involve me.

Mom lays the pad on the table and reaches into her box again. This time, she pulls out a hunk of Styrofoam and an instrument that looks like a torture device.

"I like to make a model out of this stuff first," she says, holding up the white Styrofoam. "I use a macchinetta to measure for where and how deep to carve. This kind of thing has been used by sculptors since classical times."

"The actual carving is done with hammers and chisels." She takes an air-powered hammer out of her box and shows it to the class. "At the end, for finer work, I use files and rasps. Sometimes sandpaper."

She goes on a little more about foundries and casting and bronze, and then begins showing photos of her work—sculptures of a child with Down syndrome, a pregnant woman without arms, conjoined twins.

"So often, images of people with different kinds of bodies are used to induce pity," Mom says.

A few gazes slide my way, and I can sense others trying not to look at me. Even Chad starts to squirm a little.

"Have you seen those telethons where kids in braces and wheelchairs are paraded on the screen?" Mom continues. "The idea is to make people feel sorry for them. My goal is to show the human form in its infinite variety and remind people that all bodies are beautiful."

Here is my moment. I raise my hand.

Mr. Hodge seems puzzled, but he calls on me anyway. "Yes, Aiko?"

"May I use the hall pass?"

The corner of his mouth twitches. I can tell he's annoyed, but he hands it over. What's he going to do? He can't exactly chew me out with Mom right there. And she's in artist mode, so it's not like she's not going to scold me.

I grab my backpack, sling it over my shoulder, and head out the door.

Mr. Hodge puts out another call for questions, and then everyone's looking at Mom again.

The hallway is deserted. Good. I pull the zipper on my backpack and reach inside. I grab a handful of the latest issue of *Gadget Girl* and leave a few on the windowsill. I tuck a copy into the potted plant next to the drinking fountain, and then push through the door to the girls' bathroom and leave a pile on the counter, hoping they don't get wet. Out in the hallway again, I listen for footsteps. Nothing. I put my ear against the boys' bathroom door. Nothing, again. I slip inside and leave a few copies there, too.

When I finally go back to class, Mom is at the tail end of her presentation.

She's showing the class an image of a pair of hands sculpted into the ASL sign for "love." Good. I missed *Aiko, En Pointe* and *The Birthday Series*. Or maybe she didn't show them at all.

6

After the bell, Mom takes a look at the collages on the wall. She pauses politely before each one, nodding slightly, as if she's been struck by some deep insight in "Blue Chad" or "Summer Sky," as if we are all mini Monets soon to be immortalized in museum collections. When she gets to mine, her shoulders sag. She tosses back her hair in a show of nonchalance, but I know better. She doesn't like it when I bring up my father in conversation. Nor, it seems, in my art.

She doesn't say anything to me, though. Not then. Instead, she corners me and whispers, "I'm going to have a cup of coffee with Mr. Hodge in the faculty lounge. I'll be waiting in the parking lot after school to give you a ride home."

"Okay," I say. "See you."

Next is English, the last class of the day. Whitney has the seat next to mine.

"How did it go?" she asks.

"Could have been worse," I say. "At least she didn't

wear one of her artist outfits." When she holds an exhibit, she always shows up in caftans and turbans or outrageous gowns.

"I think your mom has great fashion sense," she says.

I roll my eyes. Sometimes I wish she was frumpy and fat. And I wish she didn't try so hard to stand out. In books and movies, Japanese women are always polite and demure. I often wonder if Mom had been more low-key and didn't try to draw so much attention to herself, if my parents would still be together. And then maybe we'd all be living in Japan, where my Asian looks would be normal, not like here where just about everyone is descended from the Dutch or the Poles. The only minority students in the eighth grade are me, Linda Green, who was adopted as a baby from Korea, and Jason Tran, whose parents were boat people from Vietnam.

Being an artist myself, I understand my mother's need to create. And I get that if not for her art, we might be foraging for roots and berries. Those sculptures put food on the table and clothes on my back. But wouldn't it be cool if she could have a dual identity? Sort of like Clark Kent/Superman or Selina Kyle/Catwoman? Or even Lisa Cook, the high school girl in my magnum opus who morphs into Gadget Girl when her superheroine skills are needed? My mother could be an ordinary mom when she picks me up from school, and switch into some flashy wig and costume when she changes the world with her sculptures.

I know that it's possible to make a splash while keeping a low profile. *Gadget Girl*'s month-old web page already has 250 hits, but I only printed one hundred copies of the last edition. No one knows that I'm her creator. Well, except for Whitney, that is. And her brother, Nathan. Of course people are curious. They want to know who's drawing the manga. They post questions: "Are you male or female?" "Where do you live?" But I never reply. I like being mysterious. Plus, my life is nobody's business. I'd rather have the work speak for itself.

In the same way, I'm sure Mom's work could get by without her evening gowns and her magazine interviews. I'll bet if she tried hard enough, she could blend in here. I'll bet if she toned her act down and I learned how not to limp, we could even fit in over in Japan.

7

That evening, as soon as we finish dinner, Mom rushes to turn on the stereo.

"It's time for Raoul's show." She turns up the volume and we hear the intro music to "Around the World with Raoul."

"Good evening." His voice is smooth and mellow. "Tonight we'll be travelling along the Silk Road via the music of the group Turku. Imagine yourself on a flying carpet, floating from China to the Mediterranean Sea, making stops along the Caspian shore, the plains of Mongolia and the Persian plateau. We'll be following the ancient trade route used to convey silks and spices."

Next, he introduces the different instruments that we will be hearing—an oud and a saz (which are kind of like lutes), zils (also known as finger cymbals), and the violin. He explains that the first song is a traditional spoon dance celebrating the grape harvest in Anatolia.

I wonder if there is a Japanese song for the indigo harvest. I wonder if my little seed would like this music. I hurry to my room to get my pot. Maybe the vibrations will cause it to sprout. I put it in front of a speaker.

"How's it doing?" Mom asks. Although she doesn't know of my farm girl ambitions, she knows about my plant. She even helped me find the seeds.

"Still waiting," I say.

She sticks her finger in the dirt and loosens it up a bit. Maybe that'll help.

We set the table to the next song, a melody that gallops like hoofbeats. Raoul explains that it's a traditional Kurdish song from the city of Kermanshah in Iran. Note to self: check out a map later.

First thing in the morning, I take a look at my pot. Could it be? I close my eyes, then open them again. Sure enough, there is a tender green sprout peeking out of the dirt. It must love that Turkish music. Finally, I've found the secret! I'm on the verge of success!

I spritz the soil with water and rotate the planter again. It's sunny already—a great day for growing indigo.

I've learned a lot about indigo over the months of this experiment. For example, in some parts of India, people used to drink juice made from the leaves of the indigo plant to treat rabies. Also, some people think that indigo is good medicine for epilepsy, bronchitis, premature greying, and depression. Who knows? Maybe it could even help my leg.

I don't know that I'd want to drink the stuff, but if my plan succeeds, I'm going to harvest the leaves and dye a handkerchief or something. And then I'll give it to my father.

PART TWO

raoul

"I try so hard not to think that I am a stranger in a strange land. But I know that I stand out."
—Martha Raddatz

8

At lunchtime the next day, I meet up with Whitney in front of her locker. The inside door of her locker is plastered with movie stars' pictures. While she's willing to sit through Technicolor, she likes the black-and-white movies from the Golden Age of Hollywood the best. As we make our way to the cafeteria, she starts telling me about some old flick she saw last night on cable—something with hippos and Ava Gardner. I'm trying to tune in, but I'm distracted by the noises behind us—shhhhh-thump! shhhh-thump! followed by the laughter of boys. Without even looking, I know that a couple of jocks are at our backs, imitating my imperfect gait, the slight drag of my left leg before I plant it firmly down.

Whitney suddenly goes silent, and I realize that she's become aware of them, too. Most of the time we don't talk about my limp. We pretend that it doesn't matter, that we're both basically the same. But at times like this, the fantasy evaporates. I don't need to look at her to know that the sparkle has faded from her eyes.

"Just ignore them," I whisper.

Which would be easy to do if my bum leg didn't choose that exact moment to give way. Great.

Whitney grabs for my arm, but she's too late. All of a sudden, I'm down on the parquet floor, my books and sack lunch strewn across the hallway, in the path of hungry students. I see someone's Doc Marten come down on the brown paper bag, crushing my tuna-on-rye. A sneaker kicks my notebook against the wall—accidental, I'm sure, but still, it's like a boot to my heart. The stream of students parts and flows around us.

"Are you okay?"

I look up to see Chad Renquist towering over me.

Where are those superhero powers when you need them? If only I could evaporate into thin air.

A couple of his buddies are standing by, elbowing each other and laughing like it's all some big joke. Those must be the guys who were making fun of me.

Chad isn't laughing. I'll give him that. He actually looks kind of embarrassed by the whole thing. But even if he wasn't the one who started it, he didn't stop it. I want to believe that he's a nice person, but he was walking with them. At any rate, this isn't the special moment that I've always wanted to have with Chad. I'd rather he just went away.

"I'll be fine," I say.

He doesn't offer to give me a hand, and I don't ask him for help. I roll over and hoist myself onto my hands and knees, and stand up by myself.

He shrugs and walks away. His friends follow. I feel a pang as I watch them go down the hall.

Lunchtime migration patterns go like this: The Beautiful Ones gravitate to the table nearest the pizza. This means Chad and his buddies—the first-string football players, the track stars and basketball heroes. It also means Madison and Shari and other cheerleader types, daughters of dentists and lawyers and bank presidents who have so many outfits hanging in their closets that they don't repeat the same ensemble for at least a month.

At the next table are the lesser athletes and the hangers-on. Some of them might be called upon to fetch more pizza for the ruling class. Some of the smarter of these kids do homework for the Beautiful Ones. For the record, Chad has always been pretty smart. His name is on the honor roll every month. I'm pretty sure he does his own homework. I guess he can't help it that he's good at everything and a god.

Off in the nether regions is where the geeks sit. The chess club members, and the kids who are into making robots. Jason Tran is a member of this group. I've seen some of these kids—boys, mostly—reading

Gadget Girl. The jocks and cheerleaders? I don't know if they read at all. Maybe *Seventeen* and *Sports Illustrated*.

Whitney and I sit with the invisibles, the bland, hyper-normal kids who get decent grades, but don't stand out in any way. Technically, with my physical quirks and Whitney's personal style (today she's wearing a red and white checked shirt tied at the waist in homage to Marilyn Monroe in *The Misfits*), we're not quite invisible, but the kids at this table offer us safe haven. We are less likely to get hit by the spit balls and other projectiles launched from the jock table if we sit here. It's a safe zone, under the radar. Except, today, for some reason, there are no seats available at the invisible table.

Then I figure it out. One of the computer geeks and his sidekick are sitting in our usual places. The boy is next to one of the nondescript girls. Except today, she's not quite so nondescript. She's wearing mascara, for one thing, and her face is all lit up. The computer guy's posture is a little better than usual. He's talking to the girl, then they're laughing and she's touching his arm. Ah, young love. I look away.

"Well, we can sit with the geeks," Whitney says.

"Yeah, okay. At least they won't bother us."

We bump past other students to the two empty chairs. No one pays much attention to us as we settle in. We're still invisible, which is good.

From where I'm sitting, Chad is directly in my line of vision. Even if I didn't want to look at him, it would be hard not to. At the moment, his hand is raised as if he is holding a football. He fake passes it, and I imagine the pigskin coming to me.

"I have a new crush," Whitney whispers in my ear, breaking me out of my daydream.

"Oh, yeah? Who is it now?"

Whitney doesn't have crushes on boys at school. Hers are no risk, painless. See, she gets hung up on old movie stars in their heydays. Most of the guys she's pined after are grandpas now or already dead. Some of them—Montgomery Clift, Rock Hudson—were gay in real life, but up on screen they were the perfect straight fantasy partners.

"Sal Mineo," she says. "He's totally hot."

"Sal Mineo? Sounds Italian."

"Sicilian," Whitney says, digging into her chicken salad sandwich. "But he was cast as a Mexican in *Giant* and a Sioux in a Disney movie called *Tonka*. Oh, and he played a Jewish emigrant in *Exodus*."

Of course this makes her happy, since she is Jewish—the only Jewish girl in the eighth grade. But why not cast a Mexican in that Mexican role? Or a Native American as a Sioux? Do they think that no one can tell the difference?

"Hey, I saw *Giant* last week on cable," Luke Parker pipes up from two seats down. "A classic film!"

Whitney turns to him. "Oh, I love that movie," she squeals. And in that moment, when her back is turned to me, I feel like I'm alone.

9

It's my turn to make dinner. First, I make rice. We have a Japanese-style rice cooker that steams the grains perfectly every time. I can measure the rice, wash it, and add water pretty much with my one good hand. All I have to do to get it cooking is push a button.

In the meantime, I do some homework, check e-mail, take a look at the number of hits on my web-page since yesterday—ten!—then go back into the kitchen. I pull open the freezer door. Cold air blasts into my face. The inventory is getting low. There's nothing but a box of fish sticks, some frozen enchiladas, a package of peas, and a pizza. Since we had Italian last night, I guess it'll be fish sticks and peas tonight.

I open the cupboard and take out a copper-bottomed saucepan and fill it halfway with water, then set it on the burner. Easy enough. I hold the frozen pea package against the counter by leaning against it. I cut the top off with a pair of scissors. The cold against my middle makes me flinch, and the bag drops to the floor, spilling a few peas. They go bouncing across the linoleum. I'll get those later. I pick up the bag and dump the rest of the peas, which are clumped together, into the saucepan. I open the package of fish sticks in the same way, but manage not to drop them. Those go onto a plate, then into the microwave.

The microwave makes everything easier. And when you're used to eating frozen food, going out to dinner becomes a huge treat. But sometimes, it would be nice to have a home-cooked meal. If I were Gadget Girl, or even a normally-abled person, I'd be able to whip up all sorts of gourmet concoctions in no time at all. I imagine rolled roasts, Chinese dumplings that you pinch together with both hands, even rice balls.

I set the table, one plate at a time, one glass and then another. When the microwave dings, I call out to Mom.

"Raoul is coming to dinner next week," Mom tells me as she sits down to eat.

"Oh," I say. "Great."

I'll finally get to meet this guy, this music professor/disc jockey that Mom's been seeing for almost six months now. But what are we going to feed him? Frozen enchiladas and pizza? Not if she wants to impress him. Maybe she'll remember to hit up the store for once. Maybe she will actually cook.

The last time we had a guy over for dinner was a year and a half ago. That was when she was dating Rolfe, the foreign correspondent. She didn't see him much because he was always flying off to one war-torn country or another. Most of their relationship played out via e-mail and phone calls, although they had a weekend together in New York, during which I stayed at my grandparents' house, and another weekend in Miami. That time I spent a couple of nights at Whitney's.

The evening that Rolfe came for dinner, the first time I met him, Mom ordered Chinese take-out.

He came to the door with a huge bouquet of roses for Mom, and a jigsaw puzzle for me. When I dumped all the pieces onto the coffee table in the living room and started to turn them all over with just one hand, he apologized.

"Why are you sorry?" Mom asked. "She's good at puzzles. Amazingly good, in fact."

She's right. By the time we sat down to eat, I'd already finished the border.

I noticed that whenever his eyes landed on me, he looked away quickly, which was odd, considering the places he'd been. He'd probably seen lots of people who'd lost arms and legs to landmines, crippled beggars in the streets. Maybe he just wasn't comfortable with kids.

After dinner, when the white cartons of moo goo

gai pan and kang po chicken had been emptied, I went to my room to do homework, but I could hear their voices coming through the register in my room.

I heard Rolfe say, "Come with me." I imagined him begging on his knees, pulling her hand.

And Mom's reply: "What about Aiko? What about school? How will she keep up her art? Her Japanese?"

I knew that she wasn't worried about my study of art or Japanese. After all, she was an artist. She could teach me about colors and clay. And I was studying Japanese on my own. For my foreign language elective, I'd chosen Spanish. Maybe she was worried that he was trying to lure us to some remote country that didn't have trained physical therapists. Or maybe she was just casting about for an excuse not to go. Maybe she was ready to break up with him.

I heard him say, "...excellent facilities...independence...be good for her."

I couldn't make out my mother's muffled reply.

Not long after that, I heard a door slam and then, outside, a car engine rev up and fade away. Then my mother cranked up the blues. It was loud and I couldn't concentrate on my homework, but I didn't ask her to turn it down.

The next morning when I stumbled out of my room for breakfast, I found a brochure on the kitchen counter. It was for some residential school in Massachusetts. The photos showed kids in wheelchairs, kids with braces and helmets and crutches, all smiling while kind-looking adults hovered in the background. I felt a moment of panic, thinking that I was about to be sent away. I'd never see Whitney again. And my mother would be off in the Congo or the streets of Baghdad. I'd only see her via webcam, or maybe she'd come back for holidays.

When I heard her footsteps coming down the hall, I put the brochure down and moved away from it. I pretended that I hadn't seen it at all. Mom didn't mention the school or Rolfe or why he had left so suddenly. That afternoon when I came home, I looked around the kitchen till I found the brochure. It had been shredded into pieces and dumped into the trash. I breathed out a sigh of relief.

We never saw Rolfe again.

I can't help wondering if dinner next week will be Mom's last date with Raoul.

10

In biology class we're dissecting a frog. Or at least Melody, my lab partner, is. I'm not so good with a scalpel, so I'm just observing. With my hand resting steady on the page, I can draw the frog's innards and label the parts. I try not to breathe in the smell of formaldehyde.

Luke is over at the next table with his partner, Jason Tran. He's obviously the designated drawer. Jason is bent over the frog in fierce concentration, while Luke keeps looking over at me. Which is odd. I've never really been on his radar before, at least not as far as I can tell. Once, when I catch him looking at me, he smiles and gives a little wave.

I look behind me, but there's nothing but a wall-length poster of a flayed human body, veins and arteries running throughout like rivers and creeks.

I nod back, but I don't smile.

When he's busy drawing, I check him out. He looks different today somehow. Although he's wearing the same nondescript khakis as usual, along with a T-shirt emblazoned with the name of some obscure punk rock band. It must be the hair. Yeah, definitely the hair. Until now, he's worn it all shaggy, but now it's actually cut so that his ears and a strip of his neck show. It looks like he's even fluffed it up with gel. I have a hard time picturing Luke primping in front of a mirror. I can't help but wonder what the deal is.

Finally, at the end of class, when we're packing the frog back into formaldehyde, Luke sidles over.

"Hey, Aiko," he says.

I'm almost surprised he knows my name.

"So," he says, cracking his knuckles. "Do you know if, uh, Whitney is going out with anyone?"

I take a long look at him. He's no Sal Mineo, that's for sure. The hair is an improvement, I'll admit, but a zit is about to explode on his forehead. Plus, he's totally lacking in mystery. He doesn't brood or curl his lip. He doesn't wear tight black T-shirts that show off well-defined muscles. He's not handsome or dead or gay—definitely not Whitney's type.

"Actually," I say, drawing out the words, "she's got a thing for someone else. He doesn't go to this school."

He fakes a goofy grin. A blush rises to his cheeks. "That's cool. I figured, y'know, that she was probably going out with someone already."

He turns away, and I almost feel sorry for him. But

then I imagine Whitney and Luke huddled together at lunch at the geek table every day while I sit across the cafeteria, forgotten among the invisibles. Or Whitney and Luke sharing a tub of popcorn in a dark movie theater while I'm home alone, staring at the ceiling.

It's for the best, I tell myself. It would never work out. But another part of me knows that I'm lying. The thing is, I don't want anyone to take Whitney away from me.

I watch Luke scoop up his biology book and shuffle out of the room, head down, shoulders slouched. And then I put him out of my head. I grab my own books and make my way to my next class.

11

When I get home, I'm surprised to find a strange guy behind the kitchen counter, peeling a hard-boiled egg. He's wearing a frilly pink apron over faded jeans and a black T-shirt that shows off a tattoo of the Virgin of Guadalupe. His hair is as short as an army recruit's, but he has a line of whiskers down the center of his chin. A gourmet magazine is open on the counter and Spanish music is playing in the background.

"Hi," he says, flashing me a grin. "You must be Aiko."

"Yeah, that's me."

I see that there's an open toolbox on the counter, filled with gadgets. Good thing he brought his own tools, because Mom doesn't have that kind of equipment. You're lucky if you can find a can opener in our drawers.

"I'm Raoul," he says.

He puts down the egg he's been peeling, runs some tap water over his hands, and wipes them on his apron. He reaches out to shake my hand.

I'm so surprised that I can't think of anything to say at first.

"Uh, nice to meet you."

I take a deep whiff: cinnamon and rum. "What are you making?"

"Chilean empanadas. I'm kind of a foodie. I like to try different things, but it's no fun cooking just for myself."

I nod as if I know what he's talking about. My mouth starts to water.

"Smells good, so far," I say. "Sounds interesting." I look over his shoulder at the array of ingredients spread over the counter: raisins, olive oil, hard-boiled eggs, beef, phyllo pastry. "It looks very complicated."

He nods. "It'll be awhile."

"Do you need some help?" It seems kind of unfair to make him cook for us, since Mom's the one who invited him over for dinner. Maybe I could heat up those enchiladas to go with the feast.

"Come back in an hour," he says, "and you can help me make the salad."

In my room, I dig the latest pages of *Gadget Girl* out of my desk and get back to work.

Chaz, who is hiking in the mountains, is seared by the breath of a dragon. His leg is burned and he can't walk. Enter Gadget Girl! She battles the dragon with her Swiss Army knife, then uses the screwdriver part to drill into the earth until it releases a spurt of milky water, which has restorative powers. Chaz looks on in amazement as Gadget Girl bathes his leg in the water. Not only do his burns disappear, but also his charred jeans are repaired!

I've just added a final wildflower to the scene when I hear the cry of "Dinner!"

Oops. So much for helping with the salad.

I put away my drawing materials and head to the table. Raoul has set out a platter of empanadas— delicate golden pastries filled with spiced meat, raisins, eggs, and olives—a green salad, and quinoa mixed with cilantro, avocado, and corn.

"It looks delicious!" Mom says.

"Mmm." I agree. This is not the place to be tonight if you're on a diet, which I'm not. I intend to pig out. Who knows when we'll get another meal like this?

Once our plates are heaped with food, Raoul turns to me.

"So what kind of music do you like, Aiko?"

My mouth is full, so it takes a moment before I can answer.

"Lately, I've been listening to a lot of Chatmonchy."

He frowns. "Chat munchie?"

Obviously he's never heard of them. Well, probably no one else around here has either. I discovered them on YouTube. I introduced Whitney to the band, but she doesn't like listening to foreign lyrics. She likes to be able to understand all the words and sing along.

"They're an all-girl Japanese band," I say. "From Shikoku."

I look over at Mom to see if mention of my father's island brings about a reaction. It's hard to tell. There's nothing dreamy or distant in her eyes, no indication that she's thinking about *Otosan*. Dad. Instead, she reaches over and touches Raoul's arm, just below the tattoo.

"Aiko really enjoys your radio show," she says, "Don't you, Aiko?'"

I make a humming noise, just to be polite.

"What's your theme next week?" Mom asks.

"I'm thinking Japanese court music," he says. "You know, flutes. *Shakuhachi*."

I doubt that he'd like Chatmonchy, with their guitar riffs and perky vocals, or Bump of Chicken or the other J-pop bands I listen to.

"Oh, wonderful!" Mom gushes. "We'll be sure to listen!"

Next Mom raves about the food, telling him that we hardly ever get to eat so well.

Try never. I wonder if he has any idea of what a non-cook my mother is. I have to agree, however, that this meal is truly delicious. Who knew empanadas were so yummy? The pastry is so light and fluffy. It melts on my tongue. And the meat filling is spiced just right with chili pepper and cinnamon.

"Where'd you learn to cook like this?" I ask. I'm so stuffed that I can't eat any more.

"Oh, cookbooks. The Food Channel. You know, here and there." He shrugs as if it's no big deal. "So, ladies. Any requests for next time?"

I look over at Mom, feeling slightly alarmed. Isn't she going to nip this romance in the bud? Wasn't this a farewell dinner? I mean, Mom doesn't usually have guys over for dinner more than once.

But instead of giving Raoul the heave ho, she runs her fingers over his tattoo and says, "Why don't you make it a surprise?"

12

A couple of days later, Mom comes into my room while I'm studying and drops a folder on top of my biology book. It's long and narrow and there are clouds printed all over it. It's an airplane ticket. My heartbeat speeds up. I'm going to Japan! I'll finally meet my father! I wonder if he'll be impressed by my command of Japanese greetings, and my knowledge of indigo. Wait till he sees how well I do with chopsticks and origami! In my head, I'm already dining on sushi and seaweed soup, but then I look inside and see that we're going to ... Paris.

"Paris?" I say. "I thought you said we might be going to Japan."

She gets this look on her face, the one that she gets when I'm not politically correct, like when I call myself a cripple. I can't let it go, though. "I could get in touch with my roots. I could finally meet Dad."

According to Mom, my father doesn't know I exist. She says that his parents wouldn't permit him to marry her because she was a foreigner. They broke up, and she came back to the States. And then she discovered she was pregnant.

"You should have told them," I always say. "They might have changed their minds if they knew a grandchild was on the way."

But Mom just goes all dark and gloomy and shakes her head. "You're better off here, where people don't carry on about bloodlines."

Still, I think she should have given my father a chance to decide on his own whether or not he wanted to meet me. I bet Dad—or *Otosan*—is really a nice guy. He'd have to be, to put up with someone like her. I've lived with this woman for almost fifteen years and it hasn't been all chocolates and roses. I can see how she might drive a guy insane.

But Raoul is pretty cool. Maybe she's cooked up this vacation as a way to get us all together. A trial run for full-time togetherness.

"I didn't get an award from the Tokyo competition," she says. She pauses for effect. "I won the Prix de Paris! I won the grand prize!"

Mom is standing before me, waiting for me to say something. You're welcome? After all, I'm her model. She'd be nothing without me, right? No, she wants me to offer my congratulations. I should be happy for her, I know. This is great news, after all. She's finally getting international exposure, and she won a lot of money, but why couldn't she use some of her stash to go to Japan? I mean, without me posing for her, she wouldn't have won anything, right? So why can't she think about what I want for a change?

"Wow," I mutter. "That's great."

Mom doesn't seem to notice my lack of enthusiasm. Or, if she does, she's ignoring it. She spins around my room, her arms crossed over her chest. "As part of the prize, a big gallery in Paris is putting on an exhibition of my work. I want you to be a part of this. You *are* a part of this. I want you there with me when I open the show."

She's had shows before in various parts of the country—solo exhibitions in Charlotte and Savannah, a couple of group shows in Chicago and New York—but this will be her first one abroad. This is also the first time she's invited me to go along. In the past, Grandpa and Grandma have come to stay with me while Mom was away on art biz. The limelight's not my thing, after all, and she doesn't want me to miss school and physical therapy. But the Paris gig is this summer, during vacation. I have no excuse not to go.

"Is Raoul coming, too?" I ask. I can just see him hanging out at the Cordon Bleu and guiding us through a thousand menus.

"No," she says, frowning. "This trip isn't about Raoul or your dad. It's about us. I feel like we haven't had a chance to do much together lately. So how about it? Just you and me in France?"

I put the folder back down. "Do I have a choice?"

Clouds seem to form over her head. Her hand hovers over the ticket as if she's about to take it back. "Well, yes. Of course you have a choice."

"Let me think about it, okay?"

She nods and gets up to leave.

We both know what I will decide. After all, what are my options? A summer of losing at Scrabble to my grandparents? Or a couple of months in France? At least it will be someplace different.

The next morning I drag myself to the breakfast table to find that Mom has gone all out. Instead of the usual box of cornflakes and bunch of bananas, I find a plate of steaming scrambled eggs and whole wheat toast slathered with blueberry jam.

"Good morning, sweetheart," Mom says brightly. She's flitting around with her cup of coffee, trying to get ready for work.

"Good morning," I mumble back. I bite into a slice of toast with jam.

Mom and I gathered those blueberries last summer at one of those u-pick places along the highway. She hung an empty plastic peanut butter pail tied to a length of rope around my neck to make it easier for me. But even though the bucket was small, it took forever for me to fill it. I could only tug the berries from the bush with one hand, and I kept popping them into my mouth instead of the container. They were so juicy and sweet! Further down the row, Mom was all business, grabbing at berries with both hands and dropping them into her larger galvanized steel pail. We filled a few buckets and came home with purple-stained fingers and ten quarts of berries. Then we brought them to my grandmother who turned them into pies and a crisp and blueberry coffee cake. She made a batch of muffins and put up jam and compote, and even made a tasty sauce that we ladled onto salmon. Mom froze the rest so we could eat them later.

She likes to pick fruit because it reminds her of her childhood when she'd gone apple and strawberry and peach picking with Grandpa and Grandma. It also brings back memories of Japan. "In Tokushima," she once said, "there are lots of pear orchards, and tangerine trees. Persimmons, too. I sometimes went to a temple near the apartment where I lived and plucked a couple of persimmons to eat."

I gasped. "You stole from a temple?"

She shrugged. "No one else picked them, except for the jungle crows—big black birds about the same size as cats."

I pictured Mom fighting her way through feathers to get to the fruit. My brave, determined mother.

Thinking of Japan brings me back to the eggs

and toast with blueberry jam, and Mom, now humming in the bathroom. She must have made this special meal by way of apology, or because she wants to soften me up. She knows that I've been wanting to go to Japan for what seems like forever, but we're going to France instead.

At lunchtime I head for the Invisible Table, but Whitney veers toward the Geeks. "Let's sit over there for a change."

Changing our dining patterns will make us conspicuous, but I follow her anyway. There are a couple of empty seats next to Luke. Whitney takes one. Could she be developing a crush? On a real live boy, as opposed to the silver screen variety? On someone who is, as far as I can tell, straight? Someone who is approximately the same age as us and still alive? Am I about to lose my best friend to a boy?

"Guess where we're going this summer?" I ask her.

"Uh-oh. You're not jumping up and down, so I guess it's not Japan."

I nod. "Nope. We're going to Paris."

She squeals. Her reaction causes nearly everyone at the cheerleader and jock table to look our way.

"Paris? You're so lucky!"

For a moment, I wish I could send her in my place.

"Hey," she says. "You can go see Delight Hubbard at the Moulin Rouge!"

Delight Hubbard is a local legend. Back in the day, she was a Drama Geek here at this very middle school. She was also a hurdler on the track team and she could sing and dance. Her future as a can-can girl was almost fated. Plus, with a name like Delight, she was a natural showgirl. She went off to Paris after high school, leaving her sisters, Joy and Hope, behind, and joined the cabaret.

"Yeah, maybe," I say.

"And you'll be able to visit the Eiffel Tower and ride a boat along the Seine. It sounds so romantic!"

How can it be romantic if it's just Mom and me?

"How about you?" I ask. "Are you going to visit your dad this summer?"

Usually, she flies out to California during long vacations to hang out with her father and stepfamily. They've taken her to Universal Studios and Disneyland and Hollywood, where they drove by movie stars' homes. The rest of the time she lounges around her father's palatial mansion. (He did well during the dot-com era.) According to Whitney, these trips are torture (except for the visit to Hollywood), but she always comes back with lots of new clothes and CDs and electronic gadgets. Last time she got a Nintendo DS. "Guilt gifts," she calls them.

Across the cafeteria table, she nods, but she doesn't look happy. Her mouth twists into a grimace.

I brace myself for bad news. Is she going to go to

live with him permanently? Is her stepmother pregnant again?

"I'll probably be digging up grubs for my dinner,"
she finally says. "My dad has decided we're all going
off the grid this summer. He's taking us on a 'depriva-
tion vacation.' We have to hike fifteen miles just to
get to our little cabin in the woods. And once we get
there, we have to pump our own water if we want to
take a shower." She shakes her head. "I hope we don't
run out of toilet paper."

I laugh, feeling relieved. And a little bit jealous. She
gets to spend summer vacation with her father, while
I've never even met mine. I'd be happy to spend the
entire vacation hunkered down in the indigo fields if
it meant I could be with my dad. "It might be fun,"
I say. "Think about it. You'll be singing around the
campfire and roasting marshmallows for s'mores..."

She shakes her head vigorously, her dangly earrings whipping the sides of her face. "No, no. You
don't get it. He thinks my brother and I are too soft.
He wants us to endure some sort of quest."

"Well, it's only for a month or two," I say. If she's
going to be in the woods, I can hardly complain
about a hotel in Paris, even though I can barely stand
the thought of not being able to e-mail her. To help
her feel better, I ask what she wants me to bring her
back from France.

Her eyes go all sparkly again. "Oooh, I don't know.

A snowglobe of the Eiffel Tower? Or maybe a scarf? French women are so good with scarves."

"Okay," I say, "one scarf and one snow globe coming up. By the way, when you're out there hiking around, keep your mouth open."

"Why?" she asks, wrinkling her nose. She's probably imagining flies landing on her tongue. But I'm thinking of Lisa Cook in the mountains, swallowing a star and becoming a superheroine.

13

The next time Raoul comes over, he whips up a fabulous veal marsala. We stuff ourselves, and then he asks if he can take my mother and me out for a cup of organically brewed Guatemala Antigua at the anarchist café. Oh, and for a bit of folk music, too—a local singer/songwriter with an acoustic guitar is headlining tonight. Raoul is always on the listen for something new.

"It's warm tonight. We can put the top down on my convertible." I'd love to ride in his car, but I'm not really in the mood to go out tonight.

"You kids go ahead," I say. "I've still got homework. Just don't keep Mom out too late."

We all load the dishwasher together, and then I shoo them out the door. I work on a paper for English class, then watch TV for a little while and check my e-mail. There's a message from a girl named Brandy who lives in Alaska. I sent a copy of *Gadget Girl* to her as a trade for her comic, *Moose!* I read about it in *Broken Pencil*, a magazine that reviews zines. There's also some fan mail from Zack in Tallahassee, author of *Gator Gothic*. Happily, the *Gadget Girl* website has had ten more hits since I last checked two nights ago. I answer my messages and go to bed feeling all warm and happy.

In the morning I find a copy of the latest *Gadget Girl* on the table, alongside the newspaper.

"Good morning," Mom says. She's at the counter slicing fruit. She sees me noticing the comic. "We picked that up last night at the café. Raoul is a big fan."

"No kidding?"

She's got her eyes on her me, as if she's waiting for more of a reaction. "In this issue, Gadget Girl uses a macchinetta. Not too many people know what that is, do they?"

I shrug. "You always talk about it during your presentations. Maybe someone was influenced by you."

"Someone in your art class, do you think?"

"Yeah, sure. Why not?"

I open it up and pretend it's for the first time. I'm not ready to come clean to Mom about my role in this. She'd probably make a big deal out of it and pressure me to go public.

"It's pretty good," Mom says, still watching me. "Nice contrast. Great story line, too."

"Thanks," I say, under my breath.

The next day, between third and fourth periods, Whitney finds me in the hallway and grabs my arm.

"You'll never guess who's become a fan of *Gadget Girl*!"

I ponder. "Luke Parker?" Some kids call him Alien because a) he's a little spacey and b) he claims to have seen a U.F.O. land in his backyard. Not only is he a walking encyclopedia when it comes to things extra-terrestrial, but also he's a huge comic-book fan.

"No!"

Before I can hazard another guess, Whitney blurts out, "Chad Renquist!"

"Really?" Art class aside, I never would have pegged him for the manga-reading type. I wonder where he got it. I wonder if he liked it. I wonder if he's figured out that I had a crush on him. How embarrassing would that be?

"He had a copy of the latest issue in study hall today. I heard him talking with his friends. They've noticed a certain similarity between Chaz Whittaker and you-know-who."

I take a look around, make sure no one's listening in on our conversation, then lower my voice. "Did they have any idea who the artist might be?"

"Yeah, they did." Whitney laughs merrily, adjusting the lace bed jacket that she's wearing over her tank top. "They think it's your mom."

"My mom?" Oh, no! I can't decide which part of that bothers me the most—the idea that my mother is getting credit for my work, or the notion that my thirty-eight-year-old mother would have found her muse in Chad Renquist. I'm going to have to do something about this, but what? Have my mother issue a statement? Sign my name to the next edition? This is too much to think about now, with a trip to Paris coming up and all. I'll deal with it when I get back.

"Must have been the macchinetta," I say. "That was a big mistake."

When I get home from school, I find Mom at the kitchen table with a stack of books and our portable CD player.

A female voice says, *"Voulez-vous une chambre?"*

"What's this?" I ask, going over for a better look.

"I was thinking you could learn a few phrases," she says. "It'll make you feel more independent."

At school, we study foreign languages. We only have three choices—French, Spanish, or German. I'm taking Spanish as an elective. Someday it'll be spoken more widely in the States than English, so it's best to be prepared. Plus, I can practice with Raoul. I've also been studying Japanese with books and tapes on my own. It's pretty easy to pronounce, because the same phonetic sounds appear in English. But French. It sounds like the words are scraping at the back of your throat.

"You should at least be able to order by yourself when we go out to eat."

"*Un Big Mac, s'il vous plait,*" I say, with my best fake French accent.

Mom frowns. "Seriously. Have a seat. I've made some flash cards."

Mom was an exchange student in Avignon in college and later studied art history at the Sorbonne. One of her big sculptural influences, Isamu Noguchi, who's American-Japanese like me, lived in Paris for a while. I've heard her speak French before with her friends on the phone, and she sounds like a native to me. I figure I'll let her do all the talking once we get over there.

Nevertheless, I sit down at the table and have a look at the flash cards. She's drawn pictures of food on one side, and their names in French on the other.

"Steak and french fries," I say, picking up the first card.

"*Steak frites,*" Mom says, and I try to repeat it.

"Yum. Ice cream." I pretend to lick the next card.

Mom shakes her head. "*La glace.*"

14

The night of the end-of-the-year dance, the middle school cafeteria becomes a different place. The nutritional posters on the wall are covered up with black paper and a disco ball hangs from the ceiling, scattering light. There's a table along one wall where guys in dress pants and ties line up for punch. They fill their cups, and then heap paper plates with nuts and chips and bring them to their dates. The girls are all in dresses that show off their legs and heels. The music blaring from a stereo system set up in the corner is a mix of oldies and current hits. The girls' cologne will fill the air, masking the lingering odor of the fish burgers that were served earlier in the day.

At first everyone kind of hugs the wall. The dance floor is deserted. Nobody likes the songs the teachers picked. But then a really cool song will come on, and someone, Madison Fox, maybe, will squeal and drag Chad out onto the floor. Other couples will follow. There will be so many people dancing that they'll be bumping elbows and stepping on each others' feet. People will start kicking off their shoes, and they'll be dancing in their socks or barefoot. And then a slow song will come on, a make-out ballad, and the floor will thin out. A few couples will hug and sway to the music, barely moving while the faculty chaperones watch.

All this is all hearsay. I've never been. Neither has Whitney, and we won't be going this year, either.

"Why don't you go stag?" Mom asked me. "If you want to go, that is. You and Whitney can dance together."

"No way. I don't want to go," I told her. Next thing, she'd be fixing me up with a date. "I've got plans anyway."

My plans are to spend the night at Whitney's house. I have Mom drop me off after dinner with my little overnight bag. Whitney greets me at the door and waves a DVD in my face.

"I rented a movie," she says. "My mom's making popcorn."

On the way to her room, we pass by Nathan, who's cross-legged on the living room floor, playing a video game.

"Hi, Nathan," I say.

"Hi!" He nods his curly head my way. "That last issue of *Gadget Girl* was great!"

"Thanks," I say.

He turns back to his game and lets out a belch.

"Gross!" Whitney drags me onward. "You're so lucky you don't have any guys in your house."

"Well, there's Raoul," I say. He has dinner with us almost every other night now.

"Yeah, but he and your Mom are just dating. He's on his best behavior so she won't break up with him. He doesn't actually live with you. Believe me, if he did, he'd be leaving the toilet seat up."

It's hard to imagine that a man like Raoul, who wears an apron while cooking, would be a slob. But what do I know? Maybe when he's home alone, he's totally different.

We duck into the kitchen to say hello to Whitney's mom, who is indeed popping popcorn on the stove.

"Hi, Mrs. Goldman."

Whitney's mom is dressed in sweatpants and a big button-down shirt, untucked. Her frizzy hair is pulled into a scrunchie. She looks comfortable and, well, homey. The kitchen is comfortable, too. There's a jar of homemade cookies on the counter and notes tacked onto the refrigerator door with animal-shaped magnets.

"Hi there," she says, hugging me. "I hear you're going to France."

"Yup. Mom's got a big show."

"You watch out for those French boys," she says. "They'll be all over you."

As if. "Sure thing, Mrs. Goldman. Hey, do you want me to bring you anything? *Un baguette?* Your favorite perfume?"

"Just send us a postcard, hon. That'll be plenty."

The rat-a-tat-tat of the popping slows to an occasional burst. Mrs. Goldman turns off the heat, dumps the fluffy white kernels into a big bowl, and sprinkles them with salt. "Here you go, girls. Enjoy."

Whitney grabs a couple of cans of Diet Coke from the refrigerator and we move on to her lair. I drop my bag on the floor.

If my room is holiday-in-Japan, then entering hers is like time-traveling to the heyday of Hollywood. Her vanity looks like a backstage dressing table, what with the feather boa draped over it and the rows of lightbulbs around the mirror. The walls are plastered with posters advertising blockbuster movies—*Gone with the Wind, Casablanca,* and *Giant.* I take a good look at the latter and check out Sal Mineo.

"He *is* cute," I say. Rumor has it that he was gay. "Too bad he's dead and gone."

Whitney rolls her eyes. She's heard this from me before. "A girl can dream, can't she?"

We plop ourselves on Whitney's bed. For a moment, there is only the crunching of popcorn and the hiss of cans being opened. Then Whitney says, "I heard that Luke asked Stacy Jones to the dance."

Her voice wavers, as if she's about to cry. So she

really does like the guy. I feel a stab of guilt knowing that Luke would have asked Whitney to go with him if I'd given him any sort of encouragement. She would have finally had a chance to wear the turquoise evening gown with spaghetti straps—a copy of the dress that Grace Kelly wore when she accepted her Academy Award for *The Country Girl*—that's been hanging in her closet for a year now. But then again, she deserves so much better.

"So did she say yes?" I ask.

"I don't know." She shrugs. "Who cares, right?" She works up a smile and tosses her hair.

Obviously, Whitney cares. Okay, so maybe I shouldn't have said that she was interested in someone else. Maybe I should have told Luke that he had a chance. I could have spent one miserable night alone. It wouldn't have killed me.

"Maybe he'll ask you to the next dance," I say.

"Yeah, maybe," she says doubtfully. "Maybe by then we'll both have boyfriends."

I doubt that. We've known the same boys since elementary school, and none of them have ever expressed the slightest interest in me. And why would they? There are plenty of girls at our school who don't limp, and who don't have a hand like a claw.

"So what movie did you rent?" I ask, trying to change the subject.

She hands the DVD over. *"The Song of Bernadette.*

It's about this French girl who became a saint. In honor of your impending trip to France. Have you ever seen it?"

"No."

She sighs, as if she can't believe how uncultured I am.

I read the back of the case. "Bernadette Soubirous is a sickly 14-year-old girl who sees a vision of a 'beautiful lady,' and never suffers from her illness again."

Kind of a strange choice of movie for a nice Jewish girl, I think. I would have picked something else: Romantic comedy. Horror. Something by Hayao Miyazaki. But hey, I'm just visiting.

We shove her mountain of stuffed animals aside, get all comfy on her bed, and start the movie.

Jennifer Jones is the star. During one sleepover, we watched her in some old movie where she played Gregory Peck's sexy mixed-race girlfriend. But here she's sort of slow and sweet. She does a lot of coughing in the beginning because her character has asthma.

When Whitney's mom comes in with more popcorn, Bernadette is going to collect wood at some old dumpsite. It's here that she has her vision. Of course, no one else can see the beautiful lady in white that she speaks of. No one believes her. But she stops coughing and suddenly good things start to happen to her desperately poor family.

I wasn't raised as a Catholic. My mother has basically brought me up without any kind of religion at all, so I've never been one to believe in miracles. But a chill goes down my back all the same. What if Bernadette really did receive a vision? What if she was truly capable of curing people of their hideous diseases? What if she was capable of curing me?

I glance over at Whitney, wondering if she's thinking the same thing.

Her eyes are glued to the screen. She's so intent that she's not even eating the popcorn. I grab a handful and stuff it into my mouth.

I watch as the Empress brings her sick son to be doused with water from the spring at Lourdes. He gets better almost immediately. Maybe it was just a coincidence and the virus had already run its course. But maybe that water had special power, just like people said.

The end is sad. I feel sorry for Bernadette when she gets shipped off to the convent, and even sorrier when she dies. A few tears streak down my face. Whitney, on the other hand, is sobbing. I hold the Kleenex box while she plucks tissue after tissue and presses them to her eyes.

"That's one of the most tragic stories I've ever seen," she blurts before blowing her nose.

"Yeah," I agree. But inside, I'm feeling a flicker of hope.

15

Although hanging out with Whitney is one of my favorite things to do, I can hardly wait to get back home to my computer on Saturday afternoon. I want to do some research about Lourdes, but I'm too embarrassed to admit to anyone—including my best friend—that I might believe in miracles.

As soon as I'm secure in my room, I log on and start a web search. I find the official site for Lourdes and click onto the webcam. Maybe I'll see someone transform and kick aside her crutches, live as it happens! But no. It's totally dark. I forgot about the time difference. It's nighttime in France right now.

There are plenty of stories about miracles past, however. I read about this guy named John Traynor who got all shot up by a machine gun in World War I. He had all kinds of problems—epilepsy, paralysis—and he had to have someone lift him in and out of his wheelchair. He decided that he would go to Lourdes on some church trip, even though his doctor said the travelling would probably kill him. When he finally got there, he went into the grotto and bathed in the water and was completely cured! He woke up the next morning and bounded out of bed. He'd had a hole in his head from the shrapnel and it disappeared at Lourdes.

I feel a little bit shaky after reading Traynor's story. It sounds incredible, but there were witnesses. Proof! And he's not the only one to have been cured at Lourdes. I close my eyes and imagine dipping my stiff left arm into the water, letting the liquid dribble over my leg. What would a miracle feel like? A jolt of electricity? A ticklish tingle accompanied by the sound of bells and the flutter of angel wings? I imagine taking a step, finding my limp gone, and then running across the square. Maybe it's impossible, but I need to find out. Once we get to France, I have to find some way to convince Mom to take me there.

On the afternoon of the last day of school, Mom tells me to sit on my bed and close my eyes. I scrunch them shut and then I hear wheels rolling along the hardwood floor and a thunk as something is hauled over the threshold.

"Okay! Open 'em up!"

Et voila! A brand new pink suitcase, with a matching pink bow adorning its handle, stands in the center of my room. Not my color, really—I would have picked black, but Mom has always been big on pastels. When I was small, my leg braces were lilac-colored, or butter yellow, and the wheelchair I used up until I was seven was, you guessed it—pink.

"It's an early birthday present," she says.

"Thanks."

"You can take it to Paris."

"Yeah, okay. Cool."

She bites her lip. "Don't you like it?"

"Yeah, it's great." I open my arms and she moves in for a hug. "I love it."

Maybe if I scuff it up a bit and put some stickers on it, it'll look better.

Whitney comes over a couple of days later to watch me pack. She sits on my bed while I rifle through my drawers.

"You've gotta take some copies of *Gadget Girl*," she says. "I've heard the French love comics."

She should know. She's been taking French since seventh grade.

I layer some leftover back issues of *Gadget Girl* on the bottom of the suitcase.

"You can leave them on café tables and park benches," Whitney says. "Or in the Paris Metro. Who knows? Maybe you'll become famous over there!" She seems more excited about this trip than I am.

"Do you want to take some to the woods?" I ask,

teasing. I heap a nightgown and some T-shirts with ironic slogans on the bed.

"Ugh. Don't remind me." She holds up a shirt with a Keith Haring dog on it, then frowns. "You need a little black dress for your mom's opening. You know, like Audrey Hepburn's in *Breakfast at Tiffany's*."

I grab the T-shirt from her and throw it on top of the comics. Then I bury them under a pile of underwear. "I'll just wear jeans," I say.

"You can always go shopping when you get there," Whitney says, ignoring my comment. "Paris is Fashion City. *La capitale de la mode*."

Raoul cooks dinner the night before we leave: pasta with tomato sauce, and a green salad. The voice of Billie Holiday adds a melancholy vibe. I figure this is Raoul's way of saying that he'll be sad, all alone in Michigan, while we're eating croissants on the other side of the ocean.

"You'll be turning fifteen, eh?" Raoul says. "If you were staying here, we could celebrate with a quinceañera."

I've heard of quinceañeras, but I don't know what they involve. "Like a bat mitzvah?" I ask, thinking of Whitney. When she turned thirteen, her mother threw her a big party.

"Yes, sort of. When a girl turns fifteen, we celebrate her transition from child to adult. The birthday girl chooses special friends to be members of her court, and she dresses like a princess in a gown and a tiara."

It sounds sort of like a high school homecoming where the popular kids are crowned king and queen. Who would be in my court? Whitney, yes, but who else?

"And there's usually dancing, and at some point the girl's father gives her a pair of high heels to replace her flat shoes."

For a moment, I imagine my father flying over from Japan to give me a pair of shoes. I imagine his blue hand cupping my heel as he slides a pump onto my feet. And since this is all fantasy anyway, and unlikely to come true, I conjure up a picture of us twirling and trotting across a parquet floor. My left hand is on his shoulder—supple, not stiff. In this day-dream, I'm not limping.

In reality, I don't do so well in heels. I force my thoughts back to the here and now. "It sounds cool," I say, but I'm thinking it would probably be a disaster. I'm glad we'll be in Paris.

Which reminds me. I need a favor. "Can I ask you to do something for me, Raoul?"

"Sure. Anything."

"Would you take care of my indigo plant? I've writ-ten the instructions down. It shouldn't be too hard."

To tell the truth, I'm a bit worried about my plant.

Although it responded well to the music of the Silk Road, it has been looking a tad droopy ever since. I'm not sure what the problem is. I've bathed it in sunshine and given it a reasonable amount of water, but it hasn't thrived. I'd like to bring it along, but I'm sure the shock of foreign travel would be more harm than help. Also, it would probably be confiscated at border patrol and dumped in the trash. If anyone can keep it alive while I'm gone, I figure it's Raoul, the son of migrant workers. Considering his family's history in agriculture, he's the perfect guy for the job. If all goes well, I'll be able to harvest the leaves a few weeks after we come back from France. Then I'll start fermenting them and making the dye.

"I'd be happy to," Raoul says.

"Thanks." I'm instantly relieved. "For the record, it seems to like the zils."

"Good to know," he says.

After dinner, I help clear the table, and then prepare my fledgling plant and hand it over to Raoul.

"Have a great time," he tells me. "I'll miss you, kid."

There's a little catch in his voice, and it makes me tear up. I realize then that I'll miss him, too. I move toward him with open arms and he enfolds me in his embrace for the first time. It's warm and safe inside his arms. I close my eyes and pretend I'm hugging my dad.

PART THREE

paris

"Paris is always a good idea."

—Audrey Hepburn

16

We get to board first because I'm a gimp. Mom hates it when I call myself that, but no matter how nice you try to make it sound, the truth is I have a serious limp.

While we're sitting in the waiting area no one notices my legs. I catch the middle-aged woman across from us staring at our faces. Maybe she's trying to figure out why an Asian chick like me is traveling with an Aryan in tie-dye. Mom made that dress herself, by the way. She did some indigo-dyeing while she was living in Tokushima.

For as long as I can remember, people have been asking if I'm adopted. They think Mom is some kind of saint for taking me on. But then she says, "Aiko is my biological child," and the look turns to pity.

Written with different ideograms, Aiko means "love" and "child." Love child. In English, that means someone born out of wedlock, like me. In Okinawa, where there are lots of mixed kids from American army guys hooking up with Japanese women, *ainoko* is a bad word. I wonder sometimes if strangers think that I am that kind of child. A love child. Then again, not many people have studied Japanese. They wouldn't know the meaning of my name.

It's none of their business whether I'm adopted or not and I don't know why my mother doesn't say so. "Why are you always so open with strangers, but you won't tell me more about my father?" I've asked this a million times, and she always answers, "Some things are better left unsaid."

We make our way down the skywalk and into our bulkhead, economy class seats. Once we're airborne, I dig my iPod out of my backpack and insert the earbuds. I downloaded a couple of Raoul's shows for the flight—one of Japanese Indie rock, which he actually dedicated to me. He played songs by bands with names like "Seagulls Screaming Kiss Her Kiss Her" and "Thee Michelle Gun Elephant." The other show is of Nigerian pop.

I unfold my tray table and arrange my sketchbook and pencils. Already I'm thinking about the next volume of my comic: *Gadget Girl Goes to Paris*. I need to get the plane's interior down on paper. I figure Lisa Cook will fly over, like a normal person.

Mom pats my arm, then closes her eyes for a nap. As soon as she's asleep, I get busy with my pencil.

For the rest of the flight I read manga, watch a movie, and eat chicken. And then we're touching down at the Charles de Gaulle Airport.

After we gather our suitcases from baggage claim, we flash our passports and enter the arrivals area. Almost immediately, a honey-skinned woman plastered in a tight black suit steps up to us. Her black hair is in a pixie cut, and she is oh-so chic.

"Mademoiselle Cassidy!" she says.

"Yes," Mom replies.

"I am Giselle, Monsieur Le Clerc's assistant. I will take you to your hotel." The woman leans forward and air kisses Mom on each cheek. Mom puckers up as well.

"May I present my daughter, Aiko," she says, putting her arm around my shoulders.

"Ahh, *la muse!*"

How I hate that phrase. But I've been raised with manners, so I say, "Nice to meet you. I mean, '*enchantée.*'" And then I, too, exchange air kisses with Giselle.

"May I help you wiz zat?" she asks, reaching for my pink suitcase.

"Uh, okay. Thanks."

She grabs Mom's bag, too, and although she looks wispy enough to blow away in a gentle breeze, and I've got books in my suitcase, she manages without a drop of perspiration.

At the curb she flags down a cab and we all climb in. Soon we're zooming off to the city.

The first thing I notice about Paris is the range of colors. Though the old buildings tend toward drab grey, the skin tones on the street come in a wide variety. Whereas back in our little town in Michigan most of the girls seem to have wheat-field hair and white-as-snow skin, here there are tea-colored women and mocha men, Africans in dashikis, Arabs draped with cloth. From the cab I see Asians walking with Caucasians, black and white couples and their in-between children. I feel about as inconspicuous as I've ever been.

"We've booked a hotel for you in the Marais," Giselle says. "It's near the gallery."

"*Ah, bon,*" Mom says. "I have an old friend there. Someone I know from the Sorbonne opened a café in the area. We'll have to stop in and see him."

Okay, I've done my homework. I know that Marais is Art Central in Paris. We'll be within minutes of the Louvre, the Pompidou Center, and the Place de la Bastille, where the French Revolution began. Plus, according to my guidebook, the area is home to all kinds of funky galleries and clothing boutiques. The taxi takes us past Notre Dame, and I catch a glimpse of gargoyles.

"The hotel was designed by one of our most famous fashion designers," Giselle says. "The reception was once the oldest bakery in Paris. It is said that Victor Hugo bought his bread there."

"Wow!" I can't help myself. In our town, everything is so new. And there have never been any famous writers living there—nobody famous at all, unless you count Mom.

"The rooms are all done in different motifs—zen, Baroque, Scandinavian, modern. I believe yours is the science fiction room."

Mom is not big on sci-fi, so I can imagine her disappointment, but I'm thinking it'll be a great setting for a few panels of *Gadget Girl*.

We finally pull up in front of the Hotel de Petit Moulin. The word *Boulangerie* is still painted on the facade.

The driver deposits our luggage on the curb, where it is instantly whisked inside by a bellhop in livery. Giselle alights from the cab and ushers us into the lobby. I wait on the sofa, taking in the leopard-print pillows and crystal chandelier while Mom gets us checked in.

We follow the polka-dot carpet past black-lacquered doors and down the green corridors to our room. One wall is painted with an image of space—all planets and winking stars. In the bathroom there is a heart-shaped mirror against black tiles and a claw-footed tub.

Okay, so maybe this vacation won't be such a bust after all.

17

After we get settled in, Mom takes out a map and her Blackberry and does a little research. "It looks like Etienne's café is right around the corner from here," she says. "Wanna go have a cup of hot chocolate?"

Neither one of us slept much on the plane, but I don't feel tired. I'm actually pretty wired. And I'm curious about this friend of hers, Etienne. Is he one of Mom's old boyfriends?

We go out onto the street and it smells like no place I've ever been. There's tobacco mixed with perfume and sweat and bread. We sniff our way past *la parfumerie*, past *la pâtisserie* with its window full of delicate pastries, past the newsstand and *le tabac*. Finally, Mom stops. "This is it!" she says. We find ourselves at the entrance of a French café. It's like a scene from the Madeline books, or a movie set. An impossibly thin woman dressed all in black except for the red scarf around her neck, is sitting at an outside table. A black poodle sits at her feet, its leash twined around her chair leg.

Mom and I go inside and grab a table by the window. I'm surprised to see another dog inside—a silky blonde Labrador. A service dog? I check its owner, but he doesn't seem to be blind or deaf or otherwise disabled. The guy is sitting there reading *Le Monde*, sipping at a tiny white cup.

A waiter comes over. He winks at me over my mother's head. He looks like he's just a couple of years older than me. *"Bonjour, les jolies dames."*

Okay, I understand that. He's saying that we're pretty. He's pretty cute himself. He's got super short brown hair and sideburns that kind of curl around his face. And huge brown eyes with eyelashes like a giraffe.

"French waiters are such big flirts," Mom whispers to me across the table. She turns to him. *"Bonjour.* Is this place still owned by Etienne Brouilly?"

He cocks his head as if he's trying to process the English. After a moment, he nods. *"Oui. C'est mon pere."* His father.

Mom hands him her business card, and he disappears behind a door. Moments later, a short man wearing a white apron comes bursting into the room. His arms are open wide.

"Laina!" he exclaims.

Mom hugs him, and they kiss the air beside each other's cheeks. They rattle off a few phrases in French while I sit there, a fake smile plastered to my face. The waiter stands behind.

"Etienne, I'd like you to meet my daughter," Mom says, gesturing at me.

I hold out my hand, thinking he'll shake it, but he kisses it instead. *"Enchantée. Vous êtes très jolie."* He puts an arm around the waiter and says, "And may I present my son, Hervé. He's already sixteen. Can you believe it?"

Hervé shakes my mother's hand, and then nods to me. I wonder if he can speak English.

"Please sit, and enjoy," Etienne says. "Hervé will bring you anything you need. And now, I must get back to the kitchen. We'll catch up later, *non*? You will come to my house for dinner one night?"

"That would be lovely," Mom says, settling back in her chair.

Dinner with Hervé, I think, and my face goes tomato red.

Etienne whistles as he goes back into the kitchen. Hervé stands next to our table, awaiting our command.

"Un cafe, s'il vous plait," Mom says. They both turn to me.

"Umm, cocoa, please." Mom frowns, no doubt thinking of all the time she spent drilling me with flash cards, and Hervé isn't moving, so I give it another shot. *"Un chocolat chaud, s'il vous plait."*

"Bien." Hervé nods and slips away.

Mom smiles. "A group of us used to hang out together in cafés like this one, talking about art and love and philosophy. Those were the days."

"Did you go out with Etienne?" I ask.

"No," Mom says. "He was involved with my room-mate, but they wound up breaking up. He married someone else. So what do you want to do now?" she asks, pulling a guidebook out of her purse. "Where do you want to go?"

I look toward the kitchen, to the swinging door through which Hervé disappeared. I think I'd like to stay right here and admire the staff. But I'm not about to say that to Mom. "The Eiffel Tower?" I suggest. "The Pompidou Center?" Now that we're here, we might as well hit all the tourist traps.

Mom flips the book open to a metro map and starts to study.

Just then Hervé reappears with two white cups on a tray.

"Here you are, Madam." He sets one cup down in front of Mom, but with a little too much force. Coffee sloshes over the rim, onto the saucer, and onto the table.

"*Je suis desolée!*" His face has gone red. He deposits my cup of hot chocolate with a bit more delicacy, then grabs a paper napkin from the dispenser on the table and quickly sops up the spilled coffee.

I look down, trying to hide my smile. I know exactly how he feels.

18

We decide to do a little window shopping, saving the heavy-duty sightseeing for later. There's a Jewish bakery down the street, a star of David on its awning and a candelabra and a tray of freshly baked brioche on display in the window. There's color everywhere—blue doorways, red and orange flowers spilling over the verandas of the apartments above the shops lining the street, the red banner indicating the Picasso Museum. We come across a guy drawing Vermeer's *Girl with a Pearl Earring* in chalk on the sidewalk. Who knew you could do so much with chalk? I take a picture and then dig a couple euros out of my fanny pack and toss them into the tin can he's set out. Further along, we pop into a shop that sells old photographs and the Ali Baba Book Store.

When our stomachs start to growl, we duck into a bistro for an early dinner. It's dark and wood-paneled. The tables are covered with red-checked cloths. I order fish with some kind of garlic sauce. Mom goes for the same.

"This is great," I say, when the food comes. "We'll have to ask for the recipe. Maybe Raoul can make it for us when we get home."

At the mention of her boyfriend, Mom goes silent. Her face is flooded with what I can only call consternation.

"What happened?" My fork freezes in the air. "Did you guys break up or something?"

She looks down, avoiding my eyes. "No. He asked me to marry him."

My fork clatters to my plate. "You're kidding! Why didn't you tell me?"

"I didn't think it was the right time."

"So did you say yes?"

She shakes her head and gulps from her water glass. "I haven't given him an answer yet. I wanted to talk to you first."

A multitude of emotions starts swirling inside of me. At first, there is joy. Raoul is kind and caring and a really good cook. I can't imagine anyone I'd rather have for a dad—except for my real father, of course. And that's where the confusion comes in. I've always believed that Mom has never married because she's still holding out for my father, hoping they'll eventually get back together. And if she and Raoul do get married, wouldn't that put a damper on our plans to visit Japan someday? I could go by myself, I guess, but I was kind of hoping that Mom would show me around. Would Raoul want to meet my father, too?

Right now the only thing I can think of to say is, "What about my dad?"

She shakes her head sadly. "Aiko, I haven't seen your father in over fourteen years." She reaches across the table and takes my hands. "Your father married a Japanese woman a long time ago. They have a child— a boy a little younger than you."

Something nudges the back of my mind. My father is married? I have a half brother? Almost the same age as me? None of this makes sense. But then it does. Maybe my father was already married when he met my mother. Maybe that's why he couldn't marry her. That would mean that they were having an affair. I was probably conceived in one of those Japanese "love hotels," in a room with a heart-shaped bed and mirrors on the walls. This is all a little bit too sordid for my taste. I'm starting to feel sick to my stomach. Or is it the idea of a brother that's making me feel strange?

A brother. A cherished eldest son. In traditional Japan, boys are the ones who inherit their parents' wealth and property, who are needed to carry on the family name. Daughters used to be sold off as maids—or worse—by poor families. Girls, when they marry, join their husbands' families. In the novels that I've read, the daughters-in-law are always the lowliest members of the household. What would my father care about a useless girl when he has an heir, a son? Why couldn't I have been born a boy? But no.

Things must have changed over the past decades, even in rural Japan. This is the age of computers and robots. Japan has sent a woman into space, for Pete's sake.

"What's his name?" I ask. "My brother."

She hesitates, and I think that maybe she doesn't know. But then she releases my hands and reaches for her purse. She shows me a photo of a boy, the photo that I'd found in her wallet the night when I ordered pizza.

"This is your half brother. His name is Junpei."

I take the photo from her and study it anew. We have the same slightly squashed nose, the same arch in our eyebrows. I wonder what else about us is the same. Does he like manga? Can he speak English? Is he as serious as his unsmiling face in this photo makes him out to be? And I wonder—would he be happy to find out that he has a sister halfway around the world?

19

Half of me wants to hurry on to Lourdes, and half
of me wants to hop on a plane bound for Japan where
I can meet my father and my long-lost sibling Junpei.
But before I do either of those things, I have to go to a
party with Mom.

We've been invited to dinner with the gallery
owner. To get to his apartment, we have to take a taxi
and then an elevator that looks like a cage. It makes
a ratchety sound as we go up, and for a second I'd
rather be dragging my lame body up four flights of
stairs than risk my life in that ancient box. But then
the thing stops and we're still in one piece. The door
opens. We get off.

Mom pushes the light switch. Suddenly, a row of
doors is brightly illuminated. The gallery owner
lives at the end of the hall. I hobble along just behind
Mom. We're almost there when the light goes off.

"It's called a *minuterie*," Mom says. "The lights only
stay on for about a minute. It saves electricity."

"Hmm." I grumble a little and wait for her to press the light switch again.

Mom waits for me to catch up and then presses the bell. The door opens almost immediately and we are welcomed by Madame Le Clerc, a bony woman with long, straight black hair. She looks kind of Goth, if you ask me. She's so pale, I doubt she ever goes outside. She kisses Mom on each cheek, then takes a long look at me. "Ah," she says. "La Muse!" and she does the same kiss-kiss thing to me.

I'm trying to be gracious here, so I nod a little—yeah, yeah, *la muse, c'est moi*—and then I lurch into the most beautiful apartment I've ever seen in my life.

The ceilings are high enough for palm trees, and the walls are covered with pleated burgundy fabric. Of course, there are paintings all over. It's all dark and elegant and there are about a million vases around. They look old and Chinese and are probably worth more than our house. I'm worried that I will suddenly lose control of my arm or legs and knock them to the floor. "Uh, I think I'd better sit down," I say to no one in particular.

Mom is brushing cheeks with the other people in the room. I make my way to a velvet sofa and sit down in the middle. It'll take some work to get up again without an armrest to grab onto, but at least I'm out of range of the breakables. I try to make out what everyone is saying.

The guy with brown sideburns down to his chin is some sort of artist. I admire him for a minute, till another guy, this one with platinum-dyed hair, puts his arm around Sideburn's waist. Oh well.

The woman with the chandelier earrings is the editor for some fashion magazine. Apparently she's sending someone over to interview Mom in a couple of days.

The bald man waving a cigarette around is Monsieur Le Clerc, the gallery owner.

There's nobody here my age, and no one is speaking English. But I'm okay as long as no one remembers me and starts raving about what a great inspiration I am.

Everyone pretty much ignores me until it's time to sit at the table. Mom is seated way at the other end. She flutters her fingers at me, and mouths "Are you okay?"

I nod. She seems really happy.

A woman dressed in a maid uniform brings out the first course. It looks like some sort of meatloaf. "*Qu'est-ce que c'est?*" I ask under my breath, practicing one of the few phrases I've learned.

It's been a while since anyone has noticed me, so I almost forget that I'm not invisible. I'm a little surprised when the artist guy on my left answers.

"It's pâté," he says. "Made from goose liver."

"Oh, you speak English."

"*Un petit peu.*" His smile is like a laser beam. I feel myself blush.

I'm trying to think of something clever to say, and then I get all nervous and my arm flails and knocks over his wine glass. The crystal tinkles against my plate and a big red splotch blossoms on the white damask tablecloth. It's probably an heirloom. Definitely dry clean only.

I glance up at Mom and her mouth is an "o."

"I'm sorry," I say, sinking down in my seat. Right about now, I could really use a miracle. Remembering Saint Bernadette, I try to beam my thoughts across the country to Pau or the grotto at Lourdes, or wherever she is. *Please please please let me disappear from this place, or at least make my arm behave for the rest of this trip. Either one would be fine.* I wait for a zap or a tingle. Even a *frisson*. But nothing happens. I summon up the only other French phrase I seem to remember: "*Je suis désolée.*" I'll be needing to say this one a lot.

Our hostess forces a smile and rings a little bell. The maid rushes in once again. The mess is cleaned up and we get on with our dinner. I am careful not to draw attention to myself for the rest of the meal.

20

Mom has some spare time the next afternoon so we decide to do a little sightseeing. Since she's an artist, our first stop is no surprise—the Louvre.

"This used to be a fortress," she says, as we stand in line to buy tickets. "Back in the twelfth century. And then it was just a place for King Louis XIV to keep the royal art."

I look around and try to imagine this place back then, a few nobles in robes and curly wigs wandering at a leisurely pace among the statues. Now it's mobbed with tourists with fanny packs and cameras, all here to see some of the most famous paintings and sculptures in the world. The first one I recognize is the *Venus de Milo*.

"She kinda looks like your work," I say.

"Yeah, well, she originally had arms. They broke off."

Winged Victory of Samothrace is missing a head. That must be worse than not having arms, huh?

Mom tells me how the sculptures were painted at one time. She's my own personal tour guide. We brave the hordes and take a look at the *Mona Lisa*, which is surprisingly tiny for such a famous portrait, and then it's on to the Musée d'Orsay, a former train station that is now home to lots of paintings by legendary impressionists.

We find Monet's water lilies. I imagine diving into the cool, light-dappled water, immersing myself in indigo. I wonder if Junpei would like this painting. I wonder if Junpei likes art, or even if he likes indigo. I think it's cool that Monet had a Japanese garden. It makes me feel like we have something in common.

"He was going blind, you know. That's why his paintings are so blurry. He saw the world differently, and yet his vision made things beautiful."

We study his blossoms for a while, then move on to Degas's ballerinas. I don't like the ballerinas so much. They remind me of all the things I will never be able to do. But Mom says, "Degas was going blind, too. Can you imagine? Eyesight is one of the most important tools for a visual artist."

Just like legs are important for dancing. Well, maybe I could dance if I tried. Some sort of spastic break dance. Or just using my arms.

"How about this guy?" I ask in the next gallery. "Toulouse-Lautrec." His painting is of a woman in a white wig trying to fasten a yellow ruffle onto her costume. It's called *The Clown Cha-U-Kao*, which sounds sort of Japanese.

"Well, he could see all right, but he was, uh, vertically challenged."

"You mean he was a midget."

Mom frowns. "He had a congenital calcium deficiency. He broke his legs and they never healed properly."

If they hadn't been disabled, I wonder if they'd ever have been famous at all. Maybe they felt they had to prove something. But what about Mom? I know she's trying to make me feel better about myself through her art, but is she also trying to make herself seem special?

"Why *don't* you ever sculpt normal people?" I ask her now.

She pauses and gives me a long look. "You think you're not normal?"

"You know what I mean," I mumble. Then, "Oh, forget it." I guess this isn't a good time to bring up Lourdes.

Next we take a cab to the Eiffel Tower. We have to wait in a long line to go up it. There's a Japanese tour group in front of us. They all have patches stuck to their shirts, identifying them as a group. Their leader waves a small flag. I try to eavesdrop and pick out a few Japanese words. I wonder if any of them know my father or my brother. It's a crazy idea, I know.

Finally, when it's our turn, we crowd onto an elevator and go up to the second floor. To get all the way to the top you have to climb the stairs. So much for accessibility. Oh well. We go out onto the observation deck. From there we can see the city spread below— the grey rooftops, the Seine snaking through the city, the Trocadero, which looks like an eagle with wings spread from this angle, the Place de la Concorde. The wind is strong at this level, and it whips my hair. I can hear the *pi-po pi-po* of a distant siren, and half a dozen different languages coming from the tourists nearby. From up here, it's easy to see that we've only scraped the surface of the city. There are so many places to go, so many things to do and see. We take a couple of pictures and go back down to the ground.

"Where to next?" Mom asks.

I'm feeling a little overwhelmed. How will we ever get to know this city in just one summer? I think we need a break. We need to regroup. "I'm a little thirsty. How about a café?"

Mom nods slowly and gets a faraway look in her eye. "Okay. I know just the place." And although there are half a dozen cafés within view, she packs us into another cab and we fly down the streets to a different neighborhood, Saint-Germain-des-Prés.

We get off at the corner, in the shadow of a church

tower. I recognize the name of the café—Les Deux Magots—from a movie Whitney and I saw. The green awning and cane-backed chairs look familiar, too.

Through the window, I can see a huge vase of white lilies and waiters in black jackets and bow ties scurrying around. The weather is nice, not too hot, so we take a table outside. Mom orders a glass of wine. I go for my usual hot chocolate.

We're sitting there sipping, ogling all the tourists with their cameras and guidebooks, when Mom drops her next bombshell.

"This is where I met your father."

"What?" I'd always thought they'd met in Japan. She told me she'd gone to Shikoku to visit the places that had inspired Isamu Noguchi. Now I'm thinking there is more to her story. Maybe there's another version entirely.

"He thought I was French," Mom says. Judging by her smile, it's a good memory.

"What was he doing in Paris?"

She shrugs. "Traveling. Backpacking around Europe. His parents allowed him a year of freedom before he had to start working on the family farm. This café was listed in his guidebook."

"So was it love at first sight?" It must have been, I think, for her to follow him back to Japan.

Her eyes cloud over and she shakes her head. "I think it was this city that made us think we were in love. I think we were in love with Paris."

I look around. A couple is making out at the table next to us, their coffee going cold. Couples stroll along the sidewalk, arm in arm or holding hands. I feel a pang, like a jackknife is being dragged over my heart. Paris is for lovers, not for someone like me.

21

The following day is interview day. Mom's got people from *Le Figaro* and *Elle* coming to talk to her. Also the *Herald Tribune* and a couple of other newspapers. But first we have breakfast in our hotel room—coffee for her, hot chocolate for me, and a basket of buttery croissants for both of us.

"After the interviews, how about I take you shopping? Do you feel up to it?"

I still need something to wear to the opening. "Sure." I take a big bite of bread and watch the flakes flutter to my plate.

I figure I'll write some postcards and look at magazines while I'm waiting for her to finish up. I'll just stay out of the way and no one will notice me.

The first reporter arrives as Mom downs the last of her coffee.

"Good luck," I say, and retreat to my corner.

Mom opens the door and gets all hostessy. She hustles everyone into chairs—the writer, the translator, and the photographer, and they get to it. I manage to pretty much ignore the whole conversation.

By noon she's finished three interviews and still has a couple to go. This is all taking longer than I expected. Anyone else would be tired, but Mom is glowing from all the attention. I guess fame is a big high.

I've flipped through some French magazines and found some styles I'd like to copy, but now it looks like we won't even get to go shopping. Plus, I'm starting to get really hungry and I'm sick of room service.

This next interview is for some fashion magazine. The interviewer is as beautiful as a model—thin with perfect skin and a sleek black bob. She's wearing a sort of fencing jacket, which must be the latest thing, and a pair of tight red leather pants. The very idea of trying to work my body into those clothes makes me tired.

"*Bonjour!*" The woman kisses Mom like they're long-lost friends. She acts like she's in party mode. She looks around the room till she spots me. "*Bonjour!* You must be *la muse!*"

My hackles go up, but I nod and force a smile. "Hello."

Mom gives me a look for answering in English, but this woman isn't fazed at all. Turns out she's fluent. "Oh, you must be so proud of your *maman*. She's a genius, isn't she? Tell me, what do you think about this show?"

Suddenly, I can't stand it anymore. I hate that self-satisfied look on my mother's face, the fawning journalists, and I hate that Mom has dragged me to this place where the lights don't even stay on. I remember something that I read in a review of her work. "To be perfectly honest, I think it's wrong for her to appropriate the experiences of the disabled for her art. Maybe she should find her own subject."

There is gasping all around.

I almost immediately regret what came out of my mouth, and yet I can't bring myself to apologize. Not yet. So with as much dignity as I can dredge up, I grab my backpack and the manga I'm reading and limp toward the door. "Bye," I say to Mom. Her mouth still hangs open. "I'm going to get something to eat."

Once I get to the street, I'm not sure what to do. Then I spot that café across the street—our café—and I decide to pop in for some *steak frites*.

Hervé is there, sweeping up broken crockery, when I walk in. He nods at me and smiles sheepishly.

"Un accident?" I ask.

"Oui," he says.

It takes me a minute to get settled, and then he's there, at my side. *"Bonjour*, Aiko. What will you have today?"

He remembered my name. "Oh. Y-you s-speak English!" Ugh. Why do I have to stutter at a moment like this? Why can't I just be normal for once? I look down so that my hair will fall across my face, hiding my blush.

He laughs. "Yes. I spent last summer in New York City with my cousin. I love your country."

His accent is so cute. I want to ask him lots of questions just to keep him talking, but all I can think of to say is, "Thanks. Your country is pretty nice, too." I look up at him again.

"*Merci beaucoup.*" He smiles. His teeth are a little crooked, but dazzlingly white. "So your mother—is she coming?"

I shrug. "She's busy right now. Media stuff."

"*C'est dommage.* There is so much to see and do here."

"Yeah, well, we're staying for another couple of weeks."

Hervé nods. "Well, maybe I can take you around the city next time your mother is busy."

Be still my heart. "Oh! That would be great."

The bell above the door jingles, and Hervé looks up, taking note of the new customers.

He gestures to my table top. "*Et alors?* What will you have?"

"Uh, *steak frites.*" I know that my pronunciation is totally American, but he smiles, makes a note on his pad, and heads for the kitchen.

A woman at a table near the window is staring at me. I suddenly feel naked, sitting here alone without my mom. I open my manga and try to concentrate on the story. It's about a fisherman who becomes immortal after eating the flesh of a mermaid. I take a deep breath and dive into the pages. My mind is in this other world, this Japanese world of sea and women who can't walk on land, when Hervé comes up behind me.

"Ah, you like the manga," he says, setting the plate of crisp fries and steak in front of me. "So do I."

I've heard that Japanese comics are really popular here. "Really? What have you read lately?" I ask.

Hervé rattles off a long list. Impressive. I had no idea so many titles had been translated into French. It kind of makes me want to learn the language.

"My dream is to become a manga artist," I say. I've never voiced this to anyone except for Whitney. Being in Paris makes me feel free, somehow. I guess it's because I know that after I leave this place I will never have to see anyone here again if I don't want to.

He leans in close to me and whispers, "My dream is to be an auto mechanic and participate in the Dakar road race. But don't tell my father. He wants me to be a doctor."

As if on cue, his father calls from the kitchen.

"*Oui, Papa,*" Hervé replies over his shoulder. "I'll be right there." He rolls his eyes at me.

I smile back. *Parents. They can be so exasperating.* But then I feel a twinge. At least he gets to spend time with his father. I wonder what would it be like to work for your dad. I imagine crouching in the indigo fields, listening to mine call out my name. I picture us eating lunch together out of a lacquered bento box, my hands blue like his. What is it like to even have a father?

And then I wonder about his mother. Is she the kind who stays behind the scenes and does the laundry and the cooking? Is she slender and chic like the French women on the streets, or just the tiniest bit dowdy? I picture a family for Hervé—brothers and sisters. Pets. Lots of friends. I've imagined so much that I feel like I know him already.

When Hervé comes back out, it's to wait on a young couple seated near the door. I know that he's working, but I feel kind of disappointed when he doesn't bother to stop by my table again to chat.

I eat as slowly as possible. I'm not really all that hungry after the scene with my mother, but I want to sit here and watch him, and eating gives me something to do. Plus, the food is actually pretty good. I stretch out the time a little bit more with a cup of coffee. *Un cafe.* I'm normally a cocoa person, but it's kind of a kiddie drink, and I don't want Hervé to think of me as a little kid. I take tiny sips, pacing myself, so that by the time I get to the bottom the brew has gone cold.

And then the door whooshes open and Mom

enters, her hair all wild, her lipstick smeared. "There you are!" She rushes at me, traps me in a hug. "I've been frantic!"

"I'm fine," I say, feeling a little irritated. Yes, I should have told her where I was going, but I wish she would trust me enough to let me go out on my own every once in a while.

Mom sits down in the chair next to mine and has a look at the plate on the table. There are only a few fries left. "So you've eaten," she says.

I nod.

"You ordered in French?"

"*Mais oui.*"

She smiles. She's about to reach over and ruffle my hair when Hervé appears, a cup of coffee on his tray. "For you, Madame." He bows slightly.

"Thanks for looking after my daughter, Hervé," Mom says, as if I'm six years old and he's the babysitter.

He winks at me over her head. "It was no trouble."

"*Garcon!*" a woman calls out.

Hervé excuses himself and goes back to work.

Finally, it's just Mom and me. I remember my outburst back in the hotel room, and I feel ashamed. "I'm sorry about what I said back there," I say.

Mom sips her coffee thoughtfully. "No, I'm glad you spoke up. It's good to know what you're thinking." She settles her little white cup in its saucer and reaches across the table for my hands. "I believe in what I do, Aiko. Not everyone can speak out. I try to give a voice, a presence, to people who don't know how to stand up for themselves. But I don't want to speak for you."

I've heard this all before, and I don't think I need to hear it again, but I let her continue.

"If you feel so strongly about having your own voice, you should do something about it. You could tell people what it's like to be you."

Yeah, I could tell them how I hated physical therapy as a child, how I once flailed so badly while trying to get away that I broke my therapist's glasses. Or how I always got picked last for the teams and how my classmates called me names and made fun of my way of walking. But who wants to hear all these sad stories? Isn't it way more fun to read about fire-breathing dragons and magical elixirs? Boomeranging bottle openers and wind-powered whisks? I'd rather stick to *Gadget Girl*.

After Mom finishes her coffee and I polish off my fries, I reach into my backpack. A few copies of the latest issue of my comic are tucked inside. I haven't distributed any in this city yet, haven't found the right opportunity, but after my little exchange with Hervé, I decide to leave one on the table.

It's a back issue in which Chaz and Lisa/Gadget Girl are in Antarctica for the Polar Cap Festival. Chaz is there for the Polar Cap Cup, an extreme snow-boarding competition. Lisa is there as a tourist and an art aficionado, snapping photos of the awesome ice sculptures along the trail—Hello Kitty, a crystalline castle, a herd of glittering deer. Plus she wants to watch Chaz. Just as Chaz has completed the first half-pipe of the race, a priestlike figure on the sidelines mutters some magic words, bringing an ice man to life. But this guy's no Frosty the Snowman. He's a snow golem, and he's after Chaz! Luckily, Gadget Girl has brought along her crème brûlée torch. She'd been planning on using it to make a surprise dessert for Chaz's victory dinner, but she whips it out early to melt the golem. There's no butane left over for the crème brûlée, but Chaz is rescued once again.

I wait till Mom goes back to the kitchen to talk to Hervé's dad, then I slide the comic under the plate so it won't look like I forgot it, but that it was deliberately left there. And then, without a backward glance, I follow Mom out the door.

"Ready to go shopping?" she asks.

During the cab ride to Galeries Lafayette, which is like the Macy's of Paris, Mom tells me that we'll be dining with Hervé's family tomorrow. Remembering the spilled wine and shattered glass at my first French dinner party, I'm almost surprised that I get to go along. Then again, Hervé almost sloshed coffee on my mother, and I saw him sweeping up broken dishes. Maybe we've got something in common besides a love of manga.

At the department store, Mom and I drift from boutique to boutique, running our fingers over silks and cottons. She unhooks a fuchsia sundress and holds it up against me.

"No way. No pink." I show her a black strapless sheath.

She shakes her head. "You're going on fifteen, not twenty-five."

And I may wear a bra, but I don't really have enough up on top yet to keep the sheath in place. She's right. I return it to the rack.

I nix a yellow dress with lace straps and a red dress with a sweetheart neckline and puffy sleeves. And then I find the perfect one. It's scoop-necked and sleeveless, with tiers of wide ruffles down the front— perfect for disguising my under-developed chest. And while the soft pink version is too sweet, it also comes in indigo.

"How about this?"

She studies it for a moment, rubs the fabric between her fingers, and then flips up the price tag. "Okay."

Mission accomplished. I've got a dress for the opening.

22

While Monsieur Le Clerc's apartment was a spastic's nightmare, full of antique pottery and crystal wine glasses, the Brouilly's home is a place to relax. The chairs are plump and soft and covered with faded chintz. The paintings on the wall don't look like they cost thousands of dollars. They're mostly replicas of those you'd find in the galleries of the Louvre.

This time, I'm not the youngest person at the table. Hervé has a younger brother, Jean-Paul, who chatters away in French nonstop, and a little sister, Marie, with hair as fine as corn silk. Hervé sits across the table from me. He nods toward his brother, who seems to be telling a story involving lots of explosions, and rolls his eyes. Mom is seated between her friend Etienne and his wife. Madame Brouilly has dark brown hair, caught up in a bun, and a wide mouth that always seems to be smiling. As soon as I stepped in the door, she grabbed me and pulled me to her pillowy breasts.

We've had bowls of cold potato soup, fish cooked in broth, and now salad. All throughout the meal there has been lots of crusty French bread.

"After dinner, I'll show you my manga collection," Hervé says.

"Thanks." Does this mean I get to see his room? I've never been in a boy's room before, though I've peeked into Nathan's, which, according to Whitney, always smells like dirty socks and Doritos.

"And by the way, I think you are *un genie*."

"A genie? Like someone who comes out of a bottle?"

He laughs. *"Non, non, non.* You are a, how do you say? A genius!"

Now it's my turn to laugh. "Hervé, I think you have me confused with someone else. Like, my mother?"

"Well, yes, your mother is *un genie*, too. But it's you who has drawn the *Gadget Girl* comic, *non?*"

I glance toward my mother, who, thankfully, seems caught up in some story that Etienne is telling. Oh, good. She didn't hear. I put a finger up to my lips. "Yes, but it's a secret," I whisper. "I don't want my mother to know."

"Oh! *Pardon.*" He lowers his voice and leans across the table. "Anyway, I think it's, well... *c'est magnifique!*"

"Really?" My face is suddenly ablaze. No one but Whitney has ever gushed over my drawings before. She's my best friend, so to her, everything I do is amazing and wonderful, and vice versa. Even Mr. Hodge has been pretty reserved about my work. He gives me As, sure, but he doesn't say much.

"Thanks," I say.

"I have a question for you." He continues in the same low voice.

"Yes?"

"I'm thinking that your father is the model for Hiro Tanaka, no?"

"Yeah," I say, though that's not entirely true. Hiro Tanaka is the kind of guy I've always imagined my father to be—kind, reserved, intelligent. Solitary. But lately, my picture of him has gotten a little fuzzy. Now that I know he's married with a son, it's hard to think of him toiling away in the fields by himself. He's probably too busy playing catch and fishing with Junpei and helping with homework to ever have time to think about Mom and the family they might have had together.

Hervé goes on. "And I figured out that your mother is the model for Gadget Girl…"

"My mother?" Not really, but come to think of it, they do share certain attributes—long hair, curves, and well-toned arms. Although I've never drawn Gadget Girl with my mother in mind, maybe my subconscious was at work.

"But I wonder," Hervé continues, "who is this *mec*, Chaz Whittaker? Could he be your boyfriend *americain*?"

Is this some kind of a joke? Surely he must know that the best-looking guy at school wouldn't waste his time with someone like me. "No," I say, my face growing hot again. "He's just this boy at school who happens to be the right type."

Hervé raises his eyebrows. "And what is the right type?"

"Oh, you know," I say. "Kind of artsy, kind of quiet, but master of the skateboard." I think of an advertisement I cut out of a sporting goods catalog in which Chad appeared crouched on a board, as if he were ready to complete a half-pike.

Hervé gives me a blank look.

I laugh. To make things simple, I say, "He's the kind who only dates cheerleaders."

"Cheerleaders?"

I roll my eyes. This is turning into a social studies lesson. "C'mon, Hervé. Don't tell me you've never seen American TV. Cheerleaders are those girls who jump around with pom-poms during basketball and football games. They're always the prettiest, perkiest girls at school."

"If they are the prettiest, then you must be one of these cheerleaders," he says.

"Hardly." The red tide creeps into my face again. I'm far from the prettiest, and no one has ever called me perky. *Plus, you forgot about the jumping part.*

Hervé's mother clears away our salad plates, and

Etienne goes into the kitchen and comes back with a tray of sorbet. He places a dish in front of each of us.

I spoon some into my mouth. "Mmm. It tastes like pears." It's not chocolate, but it's delicious. The perfect ending to this dinner.

I help to clear away the table, but Hervé's mother motions me away. "You young people, go amuse yourselves. Your mother and I will wash the dishes."

Mom gives me a meaningful look, as if she knows I'm crushing on Hervé. Who could help it? He's so incredibly cute. And nice, too.

When I go back to the living room, he's there, waiting for me. *"Viens,"* he says playfully. "I'll show you where I live."

His room is at the back of the apartment. It's surprisingly neat. There are no clothes thrown over the backs of chairs, no crumpled-up bags or empty pop cans. There are posters of cars on his walls, maybe the cars that he dreams of driving across the desert. He has a laptop computer on his desk and a bookshelf filled with novels and comic books. I recognize some of the illustrators' names, but the titles are all in French.

"I was thinking maybe I'd leave some copies of *Gadget Girl* around Paris," I say. "You know, as kind of a guerrilla marketing thing."

He looks puzzled. Maybe he doesn't understand me. I try it again. "Maybe since you like my comic, other French people would, too. Maybe you could help me with *la distribution*." I say the last word with a French accent, hoping that'll help.

The room is small, and he's standing so close to me that it's giving me a buzz, like I've had too much Coke or something. If he reached out and touched me, I think I would faint.

"Ah, *oui*," he says, totally normal. "If you like, I could translate it for you. It would be good practice for me."

I put a hand on the back of the chair at his desk to steady myself. It seems better than sitting on the bed. "You'd do that?"

"Sure." He shrugs. "It would be fun." And then there's that smile again, kind of lopsided, a young Elvis curl to his lips. "*Actuellement*, I've already started working on a translation."

I imagine long afternoons sitting side by side in his father's café, turning my words into French, our elbows and arms brushing against each other's. His lips close enough to kiss. We can collaborate. We can be partners.

And then I start getting an idea for a new character—a cute French waiter with sideburns that curl and long eyelashes. And maybe a girl that he meets who looks sort of Asian, and sort of European, too. Adventure. Danger. Romance.

23

"How about a field trip?" Mom says the next morning after we've finished our room service breakfast. "I've got some free time. We could go see the garden that Isamu Noguchi designed."

"I thought he was a sculptor."

"Of course. But he worked in many mediums. He designed paper lamps, too. One of the first ones that he made was as a gift to his sister."

His *half* sister, I correct in my mind. I know all about Isamu Noguchi's family. His mother, Leonie Gilmour, was an American writer who fell in love with Yone Noguchi, a Japanese poet. She thought they were married, but they weren't, not officially. She went back to America to give birth to her son, and while she was gone, Yone made plans to marry another American woman, a journalist for the *Washington Post*. But when this woman, Ethel, found out about Leonie and the baby, she broke up with him. Leonie had another child, Ailes, with a different

Japanese guy. Isamu got to grow up with his sister. They played together, maybe fought with each other. He made presents for her. I feel a little bit jealous about that part. It would have been nice to grow up with my brother.

"Noguchi designed parks, too," Mom says, continuing with her art history lesson. "Did you know he had a plan to design a sculpture that could only be viewed from outer space?"

"Cool," I say. "Where was it constructed?"

"It never got made. But you can't say he wasn't ambitious."

We take a cab to the seventh arrondissement, where there are a bunch of military-related buildings.

"Here it is," Mom says, paying the fare and stepping out of the taxi.

I follow and look up at an imposing structure, the UNESCO World Heritage Center.

We wander to the entrance of a garden. It's not all flowers and bushes, but rocks and asphalt. Here and there is a pine tree.

"This is the Garden of Peace," Mom says. "Originally, Noguchi was asked to design just the patio, but he convinced everyone to let him do an entire garden. He was the first sculptor to do such a thing."

She leads me to a platform, from which we can see the whole thing laid out below. "This is the dais.

Traditional Japanese gardens don't have this little stage. You're not supposed to be able to see the whole thing at once. Most Japanese gardens are revealed little by little, but Noguchi wanted to do things differently."

She points out the area designated for tea ceremony, where there are rocks for sitting instead of the usual tatami mats. "And see that big rock over there with water pouring over it? That's the *Wa no Taki*— the Fountain of Peace. All of these stones came from Shikoku. He had them shipped over from Japan."

These rocks are from the island where my father and Junpei live. I suddenly feel connected to this place.

We step off the dais and amble along the path, checking out cherry and plum trees and bamboo and magnolias. Little streams run through the garden in imitation of rivers, and the rocks are meant to be mountains. Across one stream, there are stepping stones. Mom holds my hand as I make my way across.

"See those smaller stones?" she asks, indicating three rocks in the water. "Those are *tsue ishi*. They're for resting a cane or walking stick while you cross the stream."

I never thought a garden could be a work of art before. I love all the little surprises—the pond shaped like the ideogram for heart, the three tall stones which represent Buddha and two disciples. And I'm so glad Mom is here to make sense of everything.

I like knowing that Noguchi did a lot of different things. Maybe I can be a manga artist and an indigo farmer, too. Noguchi combined plants and art. Why not? I can be American and Japanese. Maybe I can even come back and live in Paris one day.

When we come back from our expedition, I can see Hervé through the café window. He's wiping down a table by the door.

"Shall we stop in for some hot chocolate?" Mom asks. "I could use a cup of coffee."

"Okay." I lower my eyes, trying not betray my pleasure at seeing Hervé.

The bell jangles as we push the door open. Butterflies rise up in my stomach.

He looks up and smiles. *"Bonjour!"*

I'm frozen for a moment, suddenly shy. Mom puts her hand on the small of my back and ushers me inside. Great. Now I look like an invalid, like someone who needs help getting across the room. I try to shrug away from her.

Just then I hear a high-pitched voice squeal, "Hervé!"

I glance across the café. It's obviously not coming from that elderly woman's lapdog, shrill though the thing may be. And then I notice the table of French girls against the wall. They look to be around the same age as Hervé, maybe sixteen. They obviously know him. When he goes over to their table, he flicks his towel playfully. A girl with a high ponytail and puffed up glossy lips, hooks her hand over his elbow.

"Looks like our Hervé is quite the ladies' man," Mom says in a low voice.

I remember what she said that first day about French waiters. Maybe he flirts with every female that comes in here. Maybe he makes every girl feel special, but I'm the only one stupid enough to think his attention means something.

The girls rise at once, and Hervé leans in toward Ponytail. They kiss, twice on each cheek. He doesn't kiss the other two. He's never done that to me. That girl must be a good friend or more. And so what am I to him? A tourist, I guess. A customer. His father's friend's daughter.

"You know what? I think I'll skip that hot chocolate," I say. "My stomach feels a little strange."

"Oh, dear. Did you catch a bug?" She puts her palm on my forehead and frowns. "You don't seem to have a fever."

"Something I ate, I guess."

"I'll go with you." She starts to get up, but I shake my head. Right now I need some time alone.

Back in our room, I open my laptop and check my e-mail. Still no word from Whitney. I imagine her wandering in the woods, holding her cell phone to the sky, trying to pick up a signal. There are a dozen messages from people I've never heard of with the subject "Gadget Girl." One girl wonders if Gadget Girl and Chaz will ever lock lips, but writes that she loves the story no matter what. And a guy wants to know when the next issue will come out, and how he can get his hands on all of the previous ones. The fan mail makes me feel a little better. There's also one from *Broken Pencil*. I click it open and find a glowing review of my manga. "Quirky," the reviewer writes, "drawn in an appealing faux naïf style." He likes the storyline, too. This is so cool! I wish I had someone to share it with, but Whitney is the only one I want to tell.

It's funny, but since we arrived in Paris I haven't felt like drawing Gadget Girl and Chaz Whittaker. Nor Hiro Tanaka, for that matter. Instead of the heroic hermit I'd originally imagined, I'm thinking now he's more like the Wizard of Oz—a cowardly guy who hides behind a made-up facade. I feel like digging up all of his plants and leaving him on his own, but that story wouldn't make sense. I'm totally blocked. Just when my superheroine's popularity has peaked, my well of ideas has gone dry.

Instead of the girl with gadgets, I've been drawing a young woman with dark hair and almond eyes and a lanky guy with curling sideburns. They meet in cafés and street corners and in front of the Eiffel Tower. I don't have a story for these images. Not yet. But now, after seeing Hervé with those French girls, I think that maybe I should tear out these pages and start over.

PART FOUR

hervé

*"I found I could say things with color and shapes
that I couldn't say any other way—things
I had no words for."*
—Georgia O'Keeffe

24

When Mom comes back to the room, she's carrying a manila envelope. "Hervé asked me to give this to you," she says.

It looks about the size of my comic book. I guess he's giving it back. I take the envelope and toss it on top of my suitcase.

"Aren't you going to take a look?" she says.

"Later." I don't feel like explaining how Gadget Girl landed in Paris.

"He seemed pretty disappointed to find you gone."

I shrug. What does he need me for when he has a harem?

"What shall we do tonight?" she asks. "Do you want to go on one of those boats on the river? Les Bateaux Mouche?"

Those are the boats that Whitney thought would be oh-so-romantic. Well, it won't be romantic with my mother, but I want to get out of the hotel for a while, far away from the café. "Okay. Let's go."

The ride along the Seine is actually really nice. Although the day has been hot and sticky, a cool breeze lifts from the water and caresses our limbs. The rocking of the boat and the sound of the river lapping against the hull lulls me. Slowly, my disappointment drains away. I start to get a handle on the situation.

There is no reason to get upset about those girls in the café. After all, I have only known Hervé for a couple of days. And even if he likes me in that way, it's not as if we have a future together. I live across the Atlantic Ocean, in Michigan. I'm too young, according to Mom, to have a serious boyfriend. Isn't it enough that I've made a friend here in Paris? Someone who shares my interests and isn't hung up on my disability?

After the ride, we find a little shop that serves pastries and have dessert. I choose the *tarte tatin*, which is sort of like apple pie, and Mom has an éclair.

"Mmm. I wonder if Raoul could make this," I say, after the first bite.

Later, back in our hotel room, I pick up the envelope from Hervé and peek inside. It's not *Gadget Girl* being returned to me after all, but a French translation. Hervé's translation. He's photocopied the five pages of the story, whited out the English text, and written French words instead. At first I'm disappointed that we didn't get to work on this together.

Then again, maybe if I'd hung around, he would have come over to the table, and we would have discussed it. And maybe he'd be interested in helping translate more stories—the back issues, and the ones I have yet to write. At any rate, we've made some sort of connection, and now my manga is in another language. That's something worth singing and dancing about.

The next morning, Mom has stuff to do at the gallery. She invites me along, but I tell her I'd rather wait for her in Etienne's café. When I get there, I'm happy to see that Hervé is at work. He brings me a cup of hot chocolate and a plate of croissants before I've even had a chance to order.

"*Bonjour, Mademoiselle!*"

"*Bonjour,*" I say. "Thanks for translating my manga, Hervé."

"It was my pleasure," he says.

His voice makes me dizzy. I need a moment to collect myself. *He's just a friend*, I tell myself. *Pull yourself together.* I pick up my cup and take a sip. The chocolate is rich and warm on my tongue. It may be a kiddie drink, but I admit that I love it more than coffee.

Hervé winks, and goes off to serve another customer.

A few minutes later, he comes back to my table. "Have you been sightseeing?" he asks. "Maybe I can show you around after I finish my shift. I get off in an hour."

"Well, I-I don't know. My mom is kind of protective."

Then again, maybe that would work in my favor. She knows and trusts Etienne. She seems to trust Hervé. Maybe if she thinks of him as a guardian, my big brother in Paris, she'll let me go someplace with him. "Actually, I would love to see Paris with you," I say. "But keep in mind that I'm not too good with stairs."

He laughs again, flashing those white teeth. "Great! What would you like to see? The Eiffel Tower?"

"Mom and I went there our third day in Paris..." But it might be romantic at night, with all those lights.

"Hmmm. Have you been to the Louvre?"

"Well, yes." I wouldn't mind going there again, if it was with Hervé.

"The Moulin Rouge?"

Okay, I haven't been there yet. I remember Lautrec's showgirls and Delight Hubbard. Whitney would love to hear all about the cabaret, and maybe I can find some inspiration for *Gadget Girl in Paris* in their kicks and costumes. "Yeah, that would be fun," I say. "Let me check with my mother."

"*D'accord.*" And then he's off to the kitchen.

Just then Mom comes into the café. She spots me and joins me at the table. Hervé pops over to take her order—*un café*, as usual. When he brings the coffee, I make my big announcement: "Hervé's going to take me to the Moulin Rouge."

Mom's jaw drops. "Pardon?"

Hervé bows again. "*Oui.* If it's okay with you, Madame."

Her forehead is wrinkled. It's taking some time to process this, I can tell. "Well, you know, my daughter..."

"It's okay," Hervé says quickly. "We won't be climbing any stairs."

Mom bites her lip. "Maybe we could all go together?" she says.

Hervé raises his eyebrows. I frown.

"*Mom*," I say under my breath. "You let Whitney and me do things together without parents. Think of all those times you dropped us off at the mall, or the movie theater."

"Well, okay," she says with a sigh. "But you're taking my cell phone. And you'll come back to the hotel as soon as the show's over."

Back in our room, she starts fretting again. "Are you sure about this, Aiko?"

Maybe she thinks I'm too young to go out with a guy. This kind of thing has never come up before, so we've never had to discuss it.

"It's not a date," I say, thinking this will set her at ease. "He's just offering to show me around as a friend. Like a brother."

"I wouldn't be so sure. You underestimate yourself, Aiko. You're a beautiful, interesting girl."

Of course she'd say that. She's my mother. And while it's nice to hear these things once in a while, my alleged charms are not helping my case. It's time to beg. "Please, Mom. I really want to go. It'll be a once-in-a-lifetime experience. And remember Delight Hubbard? That girl from our town? Maybe I'll get to see her on stage!"

Finally, she takes a deep breath, closes her eyes, and says. "Okay."

I dig through my suitcase, trying to find something to wear. According to my guidebook, the Moulin Rouge has a dress code. They won't allow tourists in jeans.

The swirly gypsy skirt I packed is totally wrong, as is the cotton sundress. The only thing that might work is my new indigo dress. I lay it out on the bed.

My left arm starts jerking. Maybe Mom is right. Maybe I'm not ready to go out with a hot guy, in a foreign city, on my own. Even if it's not a date. What if something goes wrong? What if I knock over his water glass? What if I fall down?

I figure a bath will calm me. I fill up the tub and climb in for a soak. The water feels good on my legs. I lay with my neck against the porcelain until I begin to feel peaceful again, or at least more excited than nervous. When I'm toweled off, all damp and fragrant, I go back into the bedroom.

"You can borrow this necklace," Mom says. She's laid out her rhinestone choker against my dress.

"Thanks."

"Do you want to wear a little mascara? Some lip gloss?"

Although some girls at my school wear makeup, she's always harping about "natural beauty." She doesn't usually let me out of the house with anything on my face except sunscreen. I guess I'm finally old enough for glamour.

"Would you help me?" I ask her.

She smiles. "Sure. And how do you want to do your hair?"

I pull the dress over my head and sit down in front of the mirror. I keep my arms at my side while Mom paints my face. She strokes my eyelashes with the mascara wand, dabs away stray black blots with a cotton swab, and powders my cheeks with pink. *This is what girls do,* I think as she brushes out my hair and styles it into a chignon. *They sit in front of mirrors on the night of school dances and make themselves look beautiful.*

"Close your eyes," Mom says.

After I shut them, she gently strokes color on my eyelids, and then she steps back. "Okay. Take a look."

I do. The girl in the mirror is a stranger. She looks at least a couple of years older than me, and ten times more sophisticated. "Wow. I hardly recognize myself."

She kisses me on top of the head, reminding me that I'm still her little girl. "You look great."

"Well, Mom, if the sculpting thing doesn't work out, I guess you could pursue a career as a makeup artist."

She laughs, then reaches for her purse and takes out a handful of euros. "The Moulin Rouge is expensive, and I don't think Hervé is making a big salary down at the café. You should at least offer to pay your own way."

"Okay." I tuck the bills into my wallet, and put that into my macramé bag.

"Wait a minute," Mom says. "You need something a little more elegant for an evening on the town." She rummages through her half-unpacked suitcase and comes up with a black satin bag decorated with tiny beads. It's attached to a long, thin silk cord that I can loop over my shoulder. "Take this," she says.

The shoes are another problem. This dress would look killer with high heels, but I can't wear anything but flats. My braces would be the best bet—they'd keep my legs firm and steady—but of course they'd look hideous with these clothes. Most of the time, like at school, I'd rather take a risk and opt for normal footwear. No way am I wearing orthopedic support for my night on the town. I slip my feet into a pair of black Mary Janes and I'm ready to roll.

25

At quarter to six, there's a knock on the door.

"Go ahead. Answer it," Mom says.

Suddenly, my stomach is doing somersaults. It's only Hervé, the waiter, I tell myself. Mom's friend's son. Kind, gentle, just-a-friend Hervé. No need to be nervous. I swing open the door and there he is.

He's wearing a black turtleneck and black pants—and cologne. In a word, he is gorgeous. Plus, he smells great. I put my right hand on the doorjamb to steady myself.

When he sees me, he puts his palm over his heart. "*Ooh, la la!* You look beautiful."

I imagine that he is about to kiss my hand, or sweep me off my feet. I forget, for just a moment, that there is anyone else in the room.

"Don't forget the cell phone," Mom says, breaking the magic. "And you, Hervé, take good care of my daughter."

"*Oui*, Madame. You can count on me."

She follows us down to the lobby and outside to the curb where we climb into a waiting cab. I worry that I will have to bar her from the taxi, but she finally steps back and waves. "Have a good time!"

How embarrassing. From her behavior, anyone could tell that this is my first time out with a boy. If only she could be a little bit more casual. At least she didn't try to get into the car.

On the short ride to the theatre, he points out the illuminated white dome of Sacre Coeur and the long barges ferrying tourists down the Seine in the moonlight.

The red windmill at the entrance to the Moulin Rouge is all aglow as well. A crowd is moving toward the neon lights. The cab driver pulls up to the sidewalk. I wonder if I should offer to pay for the ride, but before I can get the words out of my mouth, Hervé hands him some money and ushers me out of the car, into the flow of tourists in jackets and gowns. I can feel his fingers brushing lightly against my back.

We go through the doors, into a chamber with rows of long tables lit with tiny lamps. A waiter shows us to our seats at a table up near the stage.

All around me people are speaking English with various accents. I pick out a Southern drawl, Australian intonation, Brit-speak and a Midwestern twang. It's as if we're not in France at all anymore. I feel vulnerable again.

"Are you okay?" Hervé asks, reminding me that I'm not invisible here. My discomfort must show.

"Yes," I say, straightening my posture. "Hey, is this your first time here, too?"

He smiles and nods. "Le Moulin Rouge is for tourists. We Parisians don't come here."

"A girl from my school is a dancer here," I tell him. "Her name's Delight Hubbard."

Of course Hervé has never heard of her. The cabaret is collectively famous. The girls have to blend in. Back in the day, there were a few women who stood out—La Goulue, and Jane Avril, those cancan dancers that Toulouse-Lautrec immortalized in his art, and Yvette Guilbert, who later became a famous fortune teller. (I've been reading up on this.)

"It's very difficult to become a member of the Moulin Rouge," Hervé says. "The girls must be just the right height and have just the right proportions. Also, they must be very—how do you say—?" He contorts his arms, drawing stares from the New Englanders at our left.

"Flexible," I say, helping him out.

"*Oui, c'est ca.*"

His deep voice makes the tiny hairs on my arms stand on end. I decide that I will tune out all of the tourists and concentrate on listening to him. With his words, I am firmly back in France.

A waiter comes around with a menu. There

are several courses to choose from, including the Toulouse-Lautrec selection. The painter was a gourmet. Not only did he paint women and horses, but also he concocted recipes. A man after Raoul's heart, I think. They would have gotten along well.

I opt for the Norwegian smoked salmon followed by braised sea bream and chocolate *entremets*. I have no idea what "entremets" are, but if it's chocolate, it has to be good, right? Hervé goes for the Belle Epoque menu—foie gras with figs as a starter, a main course consisting of rack of lamb, and a cocoa sorbet for dessert. I have a feeling that after this evening I will be too stuffed to eat anything at the café for the rest of the week. I'll have to come up with another excuse to see Hervé.

Once the hall has filled up, the lights go down and an emcee appears on the stage. And then it's show-time! Music blares, and dancers with feathered head-dresses fill the stage. They move in sync, and yes, their bodies are all the same. It would be impossible to pick Delight Hubbard out of this troupe of look-alike women.

Their breasts are perfect—firm and rounded. I try not to think about my own bust. Their legs scissor and kick with seemingly no effort. I try not to think about my own legs. And though I scan for Asian or multi-culti faces, there are none that I can see. I look across at Hervé, who is clearly enraptured. Of course.

These women are beautiful. And they are nothing like me.

I want to flee. Coming here was a bad idea. I'd rather be alone than surrounded by beautiful bodies. But, as the show gets underway, I forget about my own body and get caught up in the spectacle—the splendor of rhinestones and feathers, the cartwheels, the red-white-and-blue skirts, the women dressed like pink peacocks, the Shetland ponies which are trotted onstage on leashes. And then, the big water tank in which a fat snake wriggles and writhes. A dancer dives into the aquarium and swims with the serpent. It's like nothing I could have imagined.

Meanwhile, Hervé and I gorge ourselves on gourmet dishes.

"Want to try some of my foie gras?" He scoops a bit onto his fork and lofts it across the table. I lean forward and take a bite. Mmm. It's rich and creamy, soft enough to melt in my mouth.

I'm too embarrassed to feed him a bite of smoked salmon, especially with the American tourists sitting at our elbows, but I cut a little piece with my knife and put it on his plate.

In between the second and third courses, Hervé goes to the restroom. I take advantage of his absence to whip out my phone. I figure I'll dash off a quick message to Whitney. For all I know, she's still out in the WiFi-less woods, but it's worth a try. And then, while I'm at it, I send another text message, to Raoul: "Dining on foie gras and sea bream. How is my plant? Wish you were here." By the time Hervé gets back to the table, the phone is safely tucked away.

When the bill arrives, I pull out the euros that Mom gave me. Hervé doesn't refuse. He tucks the bills into the black leather folder along with his own money, and hands it over to the waiter. Okay, so this means we're really just friends. It's not a date. If he wanted me to be his girlfriend, he would have paid, right? Isn't that the way it goes in movies?

We stay in our seats until the last encore, and then rise to go find a taxi back to the hotel.

"That was great, wasn't it?" I say to Hervé over my shoulder.

He follows behind me. I can feel his breath on my neck. "Yes, but I wouldn't want to get in the water with that boa constrictor."

We are in a slow-moving line, almost to the entrance, when I suddenly step the wrong way and find myself... falling. I have just enough time to register surprise, shame, and a fear of being trampled. But before I reach the ground, someone catches me.

"What happened?" an American woman's voice asks. "Did she faint?"

"Give her room!" a man's voice shouts.

"Are you okay?" another voice asks. (This one sounds Australian.)

"Yeah, I'm fine," I say, still flustered. There are arms around my waist, helping me get back onto my feet. When I am steady, I turn to find myself in Hervé's embrace.

No one has ever caught me before. No one, except my mother, that is. I'm used to falling, used to being embarrassed in public. I'm the princess of pratfalls. I've picked myself up off the floor plenty of times. But here I am, caught, by a French god. I don't know what to say other than *"merci beaucoup."*

He doesn't let me go right away. "It was my pleasure," he says.

We are quiet in the cab on the way back to the hotel. My mind is filled with all the sights and sounds of the evening—the feathers, the rhinestones, the snake wriggling in the tank—and with the feel of Hervé's arms around me. He made me feel so safe, so protected. I know that he's just playing the part of big brother, but I can't help wondering what it would be like to stay in his arms. To sway in them, to dance. To kiss him.

When we arrive at the hotel, Hervé gets out first. He opens the door and holds out his hand. I take it and descend to the curb. I reach for my beaded bag. "I'll pay the driver this time," I say.

"Non, non, non." He hands the driver some money and ushers me to the door of the hotel. He walks me all the way back to our room, one hand lightly at my back.

"I had a great time, Hervé. Thank you."

"Me, too," he says. "Do you want me to help you with *la distribution* tomorrow? And maybe we could do a little sightseeing? I can take you someplace not so...touristy."

"Yeah, that would be cool." I say.

"Around three p.m., then? After I finish my work at the café?"

"Yes."

"*Tres bien.*" He leans in and his cheek brushes my right cheek, and then my left cheek. "*Bonne nuit,*" he says. "Sweet dreams."

His cologne is now faint, but it still makes me swoon. This time it has nothing to do with muscles or balance. Even so, I manage to stay upright. In fact, I'm almost floating.

When I open the door, I find Mom sitting by the window, a book open in her lap. Her head and shoulders droop, her mouth is in a pout. She looks lonely. For a second I feel bad for having abandoned her during our mother-daughter trip. "Did you have a good time?" she asks me.

"Yes. Hervé is really...nice." I'd rather keep my feelings about him to myself right now. But I sit down on the edge of the bed and tell her about the show—the can-can girls, the swimming snake.

She smiles a little and hooks a strand of stray hair over my ear.

"You know, it's too bad that Raoul didn't come with us," I say. "I know he says that he doesn't like to travel much, but I think he'd really like this place. The food, the music..."

The sadness in her eyes seems to fade just then, and I see that she misses him. I'm pretty sure that she even loves him.

"Hey, maybe you could invite him to come over," I say. "He might be able to get a cheap flight at the last minute on standby or something. I know he'd really love to see your show."

She nods slowly, as if she's trying the idea out. "Maybe."

I feel her thoughts shifting to Raoul, and it comes as a relief. I put on my pajamas and lay in bed thinking of Hervé holding me until I fall asleep.

26

By now, Mom's sculptures have been lifted out of their crates, released from blankets and bubble wrap, and positioned strategically around the gallery. Interviews have been published. Invitations have been sent to art collectors and celebrities. Preparations are complete for tonight's opening.

After Mom's show has been launched, she won't have to hang around so much. She's promised the gallery owners that she'll pop in a few times over the next couple of weeks, and of course she wants to see visitors' reactions to her work, but she'll be free to venture outside Paris. We can see a little bit more of the country while we're on this side of the pond.

On the one hand, I want to see more: Chateaux! The wild white horses and Gypsy camps of Camargue! Euro-Disney! And, of course, I want to go to Lourdes.

On the other hand, I want to spend time in Paris with a certain French waiter. My days with Hervé are numbered, I know. At the end of the month, Mom and I will head back to Michigan, back to my old life. I'm hoping that we'll keep in touch via e-mail, but it won't be quite the same as sitting next to him, close enough to breathe in his cologne.

I load up my backpack with the remaining copies of my comic and then go to the lobby to meet Hervé. Mom follows me down to see me off. He's standing near the reception desk. His jeans are faded to a pale indigo, and he's wearing a black T-shirt. A pair of Ray-Bans are on top of his head. Ooh, la la.

"The opening is at eight," Mom reminds me. She leans forward and whispers, "Why don't you invite him to the party?"

I'm not sure that I want Hervé to see me in the same room as all of those broken bodies. For now, I just want to enjoy being treated normally.

Hervé leads me to his scooter. "You can ride on the back? Yes?"

I nod.

"Where do you want to go?"

"How about someplace not too touristy? Take me to your favorite places."

He gets all serious for a moment, then nods. "D'accord. On y va."

I put on the helmet he offers me and then he helps me straddle the seat. I prop my feet on the running board and wrap my arms around his waist, grabbing my weak arm with my right hand. I can feel the hard muscles of his stomach through his shirt.

"Ready?"

"*Oui!*" I shout. The engine revs.

"Hang on tight!" he shouts back.

I lean against him, so that my boobs are smooshed against his back. I'm glad he can't see my face. It's embarrassing to be so close, and I'm sure that I'm blushing. But he nods, as if I'm doing the right thing, and pulls away from the curb.

I have never been on a scooter before. It feels dangerous and free all at once. The wind puffs out my shirt and whips my hair. We fly past grey stone buildings and an old woman in heels walking her Pomeranian. We zip by bakeries and tobacco stands and bookstores and a girl covered by a veil. Finally, Hervé pulls over in front of a music store. I can hear a song floating out the door.

"Rai," Hervé says. "North African pop."

"My mom's boyfriend, Raoul, has a radio show. He would love this."

I follow Hervé into the store, which is sort of dark and cramped. At the entrance there's a table covered in flyers advertising bands and shows and some D-I-Y comics and zines. Young people, some of them with dreadlocks or funky braids, hunker over bins of CDs, looking for treasure.

Hervé steps up to the counter and says something

to the clerk, a cocoa-skinned guy with a gold nose ring. Then he motions to my backpack.

I lift it off my shoulders, unzip it, and hand over the comics.

"He says you can put them on that table." Hervé starts to clear a space, but he accidentally knocks a stack of vampire comics onto the floor. They flutter and scatter, and suddenly Hervé is looking all flustered.

I know the feeling. I lower myself to my knees and reach for the pamphlets nearest me. Hervé and I reach for the one under the table at the same time, our fingers touching. Our eyes are on the comic, our fingers. We stay like that for a moment, half-hidden under the table, and then Hervé's fingers slide forward until they are covering mine, and suddenly the only thing that I can feel is the skin and heat of his palm. I look up in surprise. We are both breathing harder now. He leans toward me. At first I think that maybe he is going to kiss me, but there's no room under the table to maneuver, and there are people walking around behind us, coming to help gather the comics that Hervé knocked over. Instead, he moves his hand away from my hand and reaches for a strand of hair that's fallen in my face and hooks it behind my ear.

"*Merci*," he whispers. Then he pulls me to my feet.

I try to act as if nothing has happened. The store

clerk helps us clear a little space, and I plonk down my stack of *Gadget Girl*. I feel a surge of excitement, but I'm not sure if it's because of *la distribution* or the moment we just had under the table.

Hervé takes a long look at me as if he wants to say something important, then gestures to the bins. "Do you know French music?"

"Not at all," I say, a little relieved to be getting back to normal conversation. "Pick something out for me."

He smiles, making me go all gooey. "Okay. Something special for *la mademoiselle*."

He selects a couple of CDs for me and helps me choose some for Raoul.

I manage to find Chatmonchy and Kyary Pamyu Pamyu in the import section and buy them for Hervé.

While he's thumbing through the jewel cases, I keep my eye on the table. A couple of people go out the door, passing by without a glance, but finally, one girl comes in, pauses at the table, and picks up a copy.

I nudge Hervé. When he notices the girl tucking the comic into her bag, he grins at me. He seems almost as happy as I am.

It's a start, but I'm thinking of what else I can do. I don't want to be in newspapers and magazines like my Mom, my face plastered everywhere, but there are other ways to get the word out about my creation. I remember that chalk artist we came across our first day in Paris. I could write the URL to my website in colored chalk on the sidewalk, or even draw Gadget Girl.

I dig into my backpack again and pull out my electronic dictionary. I set it down and tap on the keys with one finger.

"Hey, Hervé. Do you know where we can find *la craie*?

I explain my idea, and we're off to a stationery shop.

Later, our fingers all dusty with pastels, we go to a park and settle on a bench. A little girl jumps rope nearby and pigeons peck around our feet.

"This is where I come to think," Hervé says.

I'm flattered that he brought me to his special place. For a moment, I pretend that I'm the only other person who knows about it. "What do you think about?" I ask him.

"Many things." He stretches his arms out, across the back of the bench, as if to encompass the world. "I think about the work I will do one day, the countries I will visit. He looks at me and grins. "Sometimes I think about girls."

I look away for a moment, then take a big breath. "Can I ask you something?"

"*Oui.*"

"Why aren't you freaked out by me? Most boys are."

"Freaked out?"

"You know, my hand..." Not to mention my limp.

Hervé shrugs. "No one is perfect," he says. "My aunt has MS for many years. Her body changed, but we remember what a good heart she has. When I see you, first time, I think you are very beautiful."

His words make me feel dizzy. Even though I'm sitting on the bench, I feel as if I'm twirling around. "*Merci*," I say, in my tiniest voice. "Hey, would you like to go to my mother's show tonight?"

27

Here in Paris, Mom's exhibition is called *"Le Corps Exquis."* The title kind of creeps me out. It reminds me of this game called Exquisite Corpse that we played in art class a while back, where one person draws a head, then folds the paper over, and the next person draws the body without looking at the head, and so on, until you unfold the paper and you've got a freak that makes everybody laugh. I'm wondering if the allusion is intentional, and if maybe there's some committee member with a sick sense of humor when Hervé shows up at the gallery entrance with a rose.

He's wearing a black sport coat over faded jeans. I catch a whiff of cologne when he bends forward to do the kiss kiss thing. Then he leans back, looks me up and down and says, "You look great!"

He doesn't seem to notice that it's the same indigo dress (with a scarf this time) that I wore to the Moulin Rouge.

Mom bought herself a dark blue dress, too, so

we've got this mother-daughter thing going. She looks fabulous in hers, there across the room, surrounded by admirers.

"I've seen that man on TV," Hervé says, indicating a French guy with long dark hair and a white shirt that's unbuttoned halfway.

"He's an actor?" I say.

"No, he's a famous philosopher. He's married to an actress, though."

"Huh." I just hope Mom doesn't drag me over to meet him. I'm doing my best to be incognito here. I don't feel like being called "la muse," and I don't want anyone to associate me with these statues. "So do you wanna look at the art? Or just go get a drink somewhere?"

He laughs. "It can't be that bad." He takes my hand and tugs me into the room. "Let's have a look."

Hervé goes from sculpture to sculpture, not saying a word, pausing a long time before each one. Mom's prize-winning sculpture is at the center of the gallery, up on a pedestal and surrounded by spectators. I feel my face heat up. I wish I could throw a blanket over the piece.

When we get to *Aiko, Fourth Position*, he circles it slowly, almost reverently. He doesn't say anything, just squeezes my hand. After we've gone through the whole show, we grab a couple of drinks and step out onto the veranda. A slight breeze whispers over my bare shoulders.

"Your mother is very talented," he says. "You should be proud of her."

"I am, I guess," I say. "But sometimes it's like she tries too hard to understand how I feel. Do you know what I mean?"

"Uh, not exactly." Hervé laughs again. "So how do you feel right now? Is it okay if I try to understand?"

I smile into the dark. I want to say that I feel like I'm waltzing through a dream, like I'm a princess in a fairytale, like I might float away with happiness if Hervé weren't holding my hand. "I feel happy to be with you," I say, without a single stutter.

And then the moment is shattered by a girl's voice. "Hervé!"

His fingers let go of mine.

We both turn to see a young woman in a short champagne-colored dress trimmed with sequins. Her hair is pulled into a sleek ponytail. Her lips are just as pouty and glossy as that first time I saw her in the café.

"Celeste!" Hervé says. "I didn't expect to see you here!" He seems just as surprised as I am.

She cocks her hip and drapes her arm over his shoulder. Her eyes fall on me.

"Uh...may I introduce you to Aiko?" Hervé says. "She's the artist's daughter."

The artist's daughter. Not his date, not even his friend. It occurs to me then that all along he's seen me as only that—the daughter of a famous sculptor. His father's friend's child. An American tourist to practice his English with.

"*Enchantée*," the young woman says.

"Aiko, this is Celeste." I can guess from the way she's taken possession of him that they are way more than just friends. As if I need more proof, Celeste rubs her cheek against Hervé's. He does nothing to get away.

I nod and try to act like I don't care, but I feel as if I've been kicked in the stomach. Of course this isn't a date. Hervé isn't my boyfriend. I invited him to come to Mom's opening, not to come *with me*. We are not together. I'm the one who misunderstood everything—the rose, his hand holding mine, that moment under the table in the music store. He was just being nice. Being *French*, I guess.

"Nice to meet you," I murmur. "I think I need to, um, go to the restroom."

I wrench away from them, grateful for the darkness that veils me as I make my way across the veranda. I move slowly, concentrating on every step. This would be the absolute worst time to lose my balance and fall.

"Aiko, wait!" Hervé calls after me, but I pretend that I don't hear him. I don't want to hear about what a nice girl I am, or how I'm too young for him, or how I've somehow gotten the wrong idea. I don't want him to see the way my lips are trembling.

I push through the door, back into the gallery, choking back tears. The first person I see is Giselle, Monsieur Le Clerc's assistant.

"Aiko!" Her brow furrows. She pulls me aside, into another small room off the main gallery with a brocade sofa, and makes me sit down. *"Ma cherie!* What has happened?"

"This guy, Hervé..." I can't finish. The dam breaks and tears dribble down my cheeks. There's no way I will be able to go back out there, not with streaks of mascara on my face and a red nose.

"Tsk, tsk." Giselle hands me a tissue. "Men! They are such trouble, *non?*"

This makes me laugh. How could Giselle, with her supermodel figure and perfect pixie haircut, ever have problems with men?

"Could you do me a favor?" I ask her, wadding up the tissue.

She nods. "Anything at all."

"Could you help me get a cab back to the hotel and make excuses to my mother? Tell her I came down with a bug, that my stomach hurts or something." I don't want to ruin her big evening. Plus, I'd rather not tell Mom about what happened with Hervé.

"Of course," Giselle says. "Let me get my things."

28

When I wake up the next morning, I lie in bed for a few moments, remembering last night. I conjure Hervé at the door, looking gorgeous and handing me a rose. And then my hand tucked in his as we walked around the gallery. I picture us wandering onto the veranda, the moonlight falling on his face, but try as I might, I can't block out the next part. *That girl.* Celeste. I sigh and get out of bed.

I find Mom sitting at the table in our room with a pile of newspapers. She's rustling through the pages of *Le Matin*, biting her lower lip. When she hears me enter the room, she looks up.

"Feel better?" she asks. Her gaze drills into me. I wonder how much Giselle told her.

"Mmm." I'd rather not talk about myself and what happened last night. "Reviews?" I ask, hoping to distract her.

"Yes," she says, brightening. "So far, so good. The critic for the *Herald Tribune* was very positive."

I pick up the newspaper she's mentioned. On page fourteen there's a big photo of *Aiko, En Pointe* with an admirer off to the side. My little feet are once again attracting attention. I skim through the article until I come across my name: "Ms. Cassidy's art was heavily influenced by the birth of her disabled daughter, Aiko."

I imagine Hervé picking up this same newspaper, and reading these words. *He won't be able to stop thinking about my disability.* But that's stupid. He's seen me. He's seen my hand, and he's watched me walk. Anyone who took a good look at me could tell that I have a disability. Still, I'm burning with shame.

"Why did you have to talk about me?" I ask, dropping the newspaper onto the table.

She reaches out and strokes my hair. "I didn't. The reporter must have dug up information about you somewhere else."

She's right. It's no big secret that Laina Cassidy has a disabled daughter. Ever since that first award-winning sculpture, my existence has been part of the public record. And maybe the reviewer was watching me last night. Maybe she made up her own conclusions.

"You know, some people never acknowledge their children with special needs. Have you ever heard of Arthur Miller? He was a famous playwright who was married to Marilyn Monroe for a while. Anyway, he had a son with Down syndrome. The boy lived in a home for many years. That little factoid doesn't even show up in his autobiography," Mom says. "Would you like people in the future to think that I was somehow ashamed of you? That I kept you a secret because I didn't want people to know about you?"

So what about Arthur Miller? Maybe he was respecting his son's privacy. It's not like his father could ask his permission to put him in his book. He might not have understood what that meant. *Why do you care about what people will think?* I want to scream. *Why is everything always about you?* But I keep my mouth shut because I know what she would say: that as an artist, she has a responsibility to promote social justice. That she is doing this, everything, for me. And besides, she could ask me the same questions. *Why do I care what people think? Why do I think everything is always about me?*

"Look, I know it's hard to have a mother in the spotlight," Mom says, taking my hand. "But here's the good news. All of my scheduled interviews and appearances are over. We can spend the next couple of weeks being tourists. It'll just be you and me, no reporters, no photographers. We'll blend in with the scenery."

I doubt that. People always notice my mother, and they always notice my limp. But I understand that there is no way at this point to undo Mom's fame. And I can't exactly erase the article and its references to me.

"Okay," I say, wanting to change the subject before she starts to lecture again.

She releases my hand, and then knots her fingers together, pleading. "I'm really sorry, Aiko," she says, "but I have a meeting this morning. Some guy from last night, a CEO. He's interested in commissioning a sculpture for the lobby of his company."

"Go ahead," I say. I'd rather be alone anyway.

"It'll just be a couple of hours, I think," she says. "And Aiko, if it comes through, it'll be good for us. I'll put it toward your college fund."

So now she thinks I'm all sullen because she's leaving me alone. Better that than the truth. I don't want her patting my back and telling me that there are other fish in the sea. I don't want her saying "I told you so," after she pointed out how flirtatious French guys can be. I'd rather sit here and stare out the window. Maybe eat some chocolate.

"Don't worry about me," I say. "I need to catch up on my reading, anyway." I do, in fact, have a stack of brand new manga waiting for me. After the sulking and chocolate, I may even crack a few spines.

"Thanks," she says, giving me a weak smile. "Tomorrow, on your birthday, we'll do whatever you want."

"Yeah, whatever." I'm hardly in the mood to celebrate.

I click on the TV and try to decipher French news while she gets dressed and made up. She hasn't asked me about last night, and for that I am grateful. Maybe she bought the story about a stomach virus. Maybe she thinks that Hervé is nothing to me.

After she leaves for her meeting, I sit and stare out the window for a while. I eat half of a Toblerone candy bar. Finally, I take a deep breath and get dressed. I should go down to the café. I need to apologize. I'm the one who invited Hervé to the opening, and I'm the one who ran away. I'm the one who created this whole big romance in my head. Maybe Hervé was just doing what French guys do—being charming and flirtatious. It's not like he pledged his undying love. And he's been really nice to me. We can still be friends, can't we? We can talk about manga and music and American culture.

I put on a pair of indigo leggings and a black tunic and then I head down. I can see through the window that my usual table is taken. Hervé is standing with his back to me, talking to the girl sitting there. I stop in my tracks when I see that the girl is Celeste. This time she isn't with her friends. It's just the two of them. They seem to be having a heated discussion. Hervé's hands are swooping and diving like wild birds, and Celeste's mouth is in a pout. Maybe they're having a fight about last night. Maybe she's mad that he was with me, *the artist's daughter*, instead of her. At any rate, this doesn't seem like the best time to pop in and apologize.

I hurry away, back to the hotel room. I open my notebook and start to draw.

29

"Happy birthday!" Mom throws open the curtains and bounces on the bed. The light is blinding. I burrow under the covers.

"So what do you want to do, birthday girl?"

What I really want to do is ride around on the back of Hervé's scooter all day with my arms around his waist, my cheek pressed against his back. I'd even be happy to hang out in the café, watching him bring sandwiches to others, if only he smiled at me from time to time. But he hasn't called, hasn't stopped by. And I wouldn't be able to bear the sight of him with Celeste again. Another option? I'd like to mope around in this hotel room all day with the blinds drawn. Maybe eat a gallon of ice cream.

"Oh, I don't know. How about we go see a movie?" I noticed theatre marquees all up and down the Champs-Élysées.

"All right! A movie it is!"

Mom is way too chirpy. She's always a little weird

on my birthday. Sometimes I even catch her crying. Not in front of me, but I might hear muffled sobs coming from the bathroom, or she'll wake up the next morning and her eyes will be all red and puffy. I tell myself it's because she can't stand to see her baby girl growing up so fast, but maybe she's remembering the shock she felt when the doctor told her I would never be normal.

I was a micro-preemie, born fourteen weeks too early, barely viable. My lungs hadn't fully developed yet, so I had to have a breathing tube jabbed down my throat almost as soon as I was born. Except I guess it should have been sooner, because I didn't get enough oxygen at first and part of my brain died.

Mom always says that it was a miracle I survived. The doctors gave me a thirty percent chance of making it through the first night. After that, the odds went up little by little. The baby in the incubator next to mine was almost four pounds, two and half more than me, but he died. I got stronger. I made it out of the hospital, and now I'm in Paris on my birthday.

Mom has already ordered breakfast from room service. This morning there is a basket of *pain au chocolat*, my favorite. There's a rose in a vase next to my plate.

Mom opens our copy of *Paris Time Out* to the movie listings and hands it to me. It seems that just about every movie ever made is showing at one place or another. The French sure love their films.

I scan for *The Song of Bernadette*, but I can't find it. Okay, well maybe one movie isn't showing here. But there's a huge selection of American chick flicks, Vietnam and Iraqi war dramas, and the latest sci-fi blockbusters, along with the local fare.

"How about a romantic comedy?" I rattle off a title.

"Oh, that sounds fun!" There's that perky tone again. I wonder how long she'll be able to keep it up.

The *cinema* is almost deserted on this midweek afternoon. We stake out seats in the third row and wait for the lights to dim. Before the main attraction, there are a few commercials. The first one is for orange soda. It features CG forest animals—a deer in a bikini, a bear in one of those diaper-like things that sumo wrestlers wear. They're all dancing around. Pop fizzes out of the bottle at the end. There's another for perfume, in which a woman leaps around a ballroom, her skirt billowing up so we can see her red panties. And one more for chocolate, in which a woman lying in bed takes a bite of her candy bar and starts moaning. *Puhlease.*

In comparison, the American movie is pretty tame, but it's a romance. My thoughts keep drifting to Hervé. In the movie in my head, we're riding in a jeep across the desert, on our way to Dakar. He's driving, I'm sketching. Every now and then, he leans over and kisses me. And because this is a fantasy, even though he's not looking at the road, the car keeps going and we never crash.

Later, after the movie, we go out to dinner. In the restaurant, Mom picks up the salt shaker and puts it back down. She drums her fingers on the table, bites at a hangnail. She looks like someone who really needs a cigarette.

She asks the waiter for a bottle of wine and two glasses. She watches as he fills her glass. He hesitates for a moment, watching for her nod, before pouring a couple of inches into mine.

"Hey, I'm underage," I say.

Mom shrugs. "The French don't care." She raises her glass. "Happy birthday, baby."

I look around the restaurant. There is no one else here my age. There are no parents letting children sip from their goblets, no kids with fake IDs. No one seems to be watching us, either. I clink my glass with hers and take a small sip. It tastes sour, with a hint of cork. I'd rather have a Coke.

It must be good though, because Mom downs half a glass in just a couple of gulps. Then she starts to talk.

"I always promised myself that when you became

old enough, I would tell you the truth about your father."

I freeze, afraid that any sudden movement will make her change her mind.

"So," she says, "do you think you're ready to hear it?"

I nod, but a cold feeling starts low in my belly.

"I know it seems uncharacteristic of me, but sometimes people behave differently when they're abroad." She sighs. "It gives you a sense of freedom, don't you think?"

I swirl the purple liquid in my glass without drinking. I think about riding on the back of Hervé's scooter, of our talk in the park, of how I probably wouldn't have even been able to look him in the eye back at school.

"Your father and I fell in love here. We were foreigners, both free in a way that we wouldn't have been at home. Things were different when we went to Japan."

The waiter arrives with our dinner, giving Mom a moment to collect herself before launching into the rest of the story.

She nods slowly, watching me. "We were planning on getting married, even before we knew that I was pregnant with you, but his parents said they would disown him for marrying a *gaijin*. A foreigner.

"You have to understand that he was all they had.

They were afraid that I would lure him away, that he would abandon the family farm, that there would be no one to take care of them. He was a good son and he wanted to obey them. He knew his duty, and he thought that if we waited, eventually they would give their consent. And then we would get married. But they were stubborn."

Here, she swallows the rest of her wine. The waiter comes over and refills her glass. After he's gone, she continues.

"Your father said that they would soften up after the baby—after you—came. But then..."

Enough. I don't want to hear any more. I have an idea of what comes next. *Please shut up*, I want to say, but the words don't come.

"Your grandmother said that your disabilities were all my fault," Mom goes on. "She said that I had brought shame upon the family. She gave me a big envelope of money and told me to go away. Your father was too...grief-stricken to disagree with her."

"So you split up," I say. My left arm jerks, rattling the bread plate.

Mom quickly moves my glass of wine out of range.

Suddenly I feel dizzy as if I'm the one who's been guzzling Bordeaux. I haven't really eaten anything, but I feel the urge to throw up. Control, control, I tell myself. Yet I want to overturn this table. My whole life has been a lie.

"You told me that he never knew about me!" I yelled.

Some diners look over. My mother starts crying. "I am so sorry," she says. "I thought it would hurt you to know the truth."

To know that my father was too weak to stick up for me? To know how my foreign mother and I were kicked out of the family?

"I want to go back to the hotel," I say. "I'm not hungry anymore." I'm angry at my mother for lying to me, at my father for not standing up to his parents, and at my grandparents for being so cold. I'm also angry at my body for not being perfect, and at my brother—my half brother—for leading the life I might have had. A torrent of fury is ripping through me. I can't possibly eat. What I really want to do is get on a plane and go home. Alone. But I know that's not possible. She's the one with the credit card.

Mom dabs at her eyes and nose with her cloth napkin. "Okay." She digs around in her purse, fishes out some crumpled euros, and tosses them on the table.

I get up and limp to the door.

I let her guide me to the curb and wait for her to flag down a taxi. We don't say a word all the way back. I can't even look at her. All I can think is that if I had been born perfect, then maybe I'd still have a family. And then I remember Lourdes. It's a long shot, but look at John Traynor—miracles happen. Just a few weeks ago, I heard about a guy who was in a coma for nineteen years. He got knocked out in a car accident. Then, one day, he suddenly woke up and started talking to his mother.

Maybe something like that could happen for me. Maybe I could bring my family together again. Or not. But it's worth a shot, and I have nothing left to lose. Plus, Mom owes me big time.

She seems to be thinking the same thing. I watch as she goes to the minibar in our hotel room and pours herself a drink. "Look, I know that there is no way I can make this up to you, but..."

Now. Here's my chance. I take a deep breath and say, "Well, there is one thing," This is the first time I've spoken in half an hour.

She looks up, surprised. "What?" Her voice is as soft as a feather.

I look her straight in the eye. "You can take me to Lourdes. I really want to go there."

She gulps, and I realize that she's started crying. "I love you the way you are," she says. "I've tried to help you to love yourself. All of my art, all of my life has been about that. Didn't you get that?"

She begins sobbing. Loudly. Her mascara is running down her face like mud. Her nose is red. She clutches at her head as if it's about to fall off. I feel a little bit sorry for her, but then I remember her betrayal. Her lies. "So are you going to take me, or do I have to go by myself?"

Mom turns to the window and looks out at the city lights. She takes a deep shuddering breath, then snatches a tissue from the box on the table and blows her nose. "I'll take you," she says. "We'll leave first thing tomorrow."

PART FIVE

lourdes

"I believe in kissing, kissing a lot. I believe in being strong when everything seems to be going wrong. I believe that happy girls are the prettiest girls. I believe that tomorrow is another day and I believe in miracles."

—Audrey Hepburn

30

I set the alarm. I want to make sure we wake up early. I want to get to Lourdes as soon as possible. I want to be away from Paris, away from Hervé and that girl. Away from that sculpture of me, away from the place where my mother met my father.

"I'll go ask the concierge if he can book us a room for tomorrow," Mom says.

I grunt, my head turned away. I just want her to go away. After I listen to the door open and close, I breathe a sigh of relief.

Night has fallen on Paris. I'm suddenly exhausted. My body is tired from our wanderings, but it's more than that. It's as if my mind is so overwhelmed by the news of my father's rejection that it wants to shut down for a while. I change into my pajamas and crawl under the covers. But I can't sleep. I lie there listening to cars honking along the boulevard, laughter from a group passing under the window, someone thumping around in the room next to ours. I close my eyes and try to imagine a deserted beach with gently lapping waves, but what I get is a picture of my father.

Does he ever think about me? Has he ever tried to find us? Probably not. He has another family, a wife and a perfect son. I imagine my Japanese grandparents showering them with gifts, while my mother and I are forgotten, a dirty secret from long ago.

It seems like I spend all night thinking about my father, but then the alarm goes off and it feels as if I'm swimming, swimming to the surface, and I open my eyes to the dawn.

Mom is already awake and dressed. She's sitting in the armchair, with the guidebook open on her lap.

"Good morning," she says.

I haul myself out of bed and pull on a pair of jeans. "So what time's the train?"

"In another hour."

I notice a small bag by the door. We'll be leaving most of our stuff in this hotel room.

I shuck off my pajama top and pull on a T-shirt. We go downstairs to the hotel restaurant for croissants and café au lait, and then it's off to the Gare de Lyon. I can't help thinking of Hervé, and wondering if he'll notice I'm not around.

While Mom's paying for our tickets, I buy a bar of chocolate and *Paris Match*. It's not like I can read the magazine or anything, but I can look at the pictures: Princess Caroline de Monaco in a ball gown. Johnny Depp at a film festival.

"Quai 3," Mom says. I follow her to the train, onto the car, and down the corridor. We slip into an empty compartment. I quickly flip open my magazine, but I can feel Mom's eyes on me. I can feel that she wants to talk. Part of me wants to ignore her for the rest of the trip, but there is so much that I want to know. She is the only one who can tell me these things. The train starts to pull away from the station.

"Does my father have a picture of me?" I ask.

Mom nods, then looks out the window. The city is fading away. She dabs at the corner of her eye with her finger. "I have sent letters and photos for all these years, but he never writes back."

That doesn't make sense. She has that photo of my brother. "How did you get a photo of Junpei, then?" I ask.

She's silent for a moment. "His mother—your father's wife—sent it."

I imagine this woman coming upon my photo, or a mysterious letter from abroad. Maybe she understood just enough to know that it was from her husband's former lover, that he has a daughter somewhere. Maybe no one would tell her about the woman and the girl, but she was curious, so she took it upon herself to find out more. Or maybe she wanted to show my mother that we are part of the past, that he has a new family now, and that we should leave them alone.

I'm about to say more, but then the train slows to a

stop and passengers get on. A trio of American back-packers crowd into our compartment. I don't want them to hear our conversation. My questions will have to wait.

As we get closer to our destination, more and more passengers board with canes or wheelchairs. I see a mother carrying a child with leg braces and a blind man who boards with his dog. Some get on with nurses or nuns.

Finally, the Pyrenees Mountains loom into view. This is Bernadette's territory. My heart begins to thud.

When the train pulls into Lourdes, we're already standing at the door, ready to get off. Mom carries a bag holding clothes for both of us. She gives me a hand in stepping off the train, and then we flag down a cab. Mom tells the driver the name of the hotel that the concierge in Paris booked for us, and we're off.

I look out the window, trying to find something familiar, something from the movie. I try to imagine Bernadette walking down these cobblestone streets, her mother buying meat at that butcher's shop, she and her sisters running over that hill. I try to blot out the hordes of tourists, the advertisements pasted to every wall featuring Our Lady of Lourdes, the plastic bottles of holy water sitting in shop windows.

"This is it," the driver says, stopping in front of a two-story brick building.

Mom hands him a few euros, and we check in to the hotel.

"The concierge says that this place is within walking distance of the grotto," Mom says. "Why don't we have lunch first, and then go check it out."

I nod.

We find a cute little bistro around the corner and order ham and cheese sandwiches. I thought I was hungry, but butterflies are now flurrying in my stomach. This visit to the grotto is making me nervous. What if I really do experience a miracle? What if I don't?

After lunch we take a look at the map and then start walking toward the site where Bernadette had her vision. We don't really need a map, though. It's just as easy to follow the group of pilgrims in wheelchairs in front of us.

Somehow I'm expecting a garbage dump and a cold stream, but it's not like that at all. The site is dominated by a huge cathedral. Of course, this wasn't in the film. It hadn't been built yet. Everyone was still thinking that Bernadette's vision was a hoax. The people who have gathered here obviously believe that she was telling the truth.

Mom and I fall in behind a long procession of pilgrims in white. Many hold candles. They are chanting. I don't understand the words, but they raise goose bumps on my arms.

Mom touches me and guides me forward. I sneak a look at her face. She looks scared.

"It'll be okay, Mom," I say. She forces a smile.

We shuffle along, inhaling incense, our bodies buoyed by faith. Then the line stops. Up ahead, there is wailing. A woman has fallen to her knees. I try to get a good look, but all I can see are her hands, reaching for heaven. Some guys who look like orderlies rush up with a stretcher. I think they're going to take her off to a waiting ambulance, but they don't. Instead, they carry her alongside the column of pilgrims. I can hear someone crying behind me. We begin moving again.

Down near the grotto, there are rows of chairs. I motion for Mom to wait for me, and then I move down to the cave, to the place where Bernadette was cured.

When I step up to the railing, my heart starts to bang. I feel my knees begin to buckle and I hold myself upright with my arms until I can control my legs again. All of my senses are suddenly acute. I can hear every bird in every tree. The world is bright; the mountains are haloed. It's just adrenaline, I tell myself. But fear grabs me by the throat. What if I do experience a miracle? What then? I'm old enough to know that everything has a price. You don't get something for nothing in this world.

Bernadette may have been graced with a vision,

but she was sent away to a convent. She died there, away from her family, from tuberculosis when she was just sixteen. Only a couple of years older than I am now.

I saw a movie on cable once about this Japanese woman with a brain-damaged daughter. She believed that if she made the tour of eighty-eight temples in Shikoku, her girl would be able to walk. Even when she was grown, the mother pushed her child from temple to temple in this wicker buggy, picking fruit along the way to earn money for food. Finally, at the last temple, the daughter got out of the buggy, stood up on her own, took one step, fell down, and died.

I take a deep breath. My heart starts to slow down. *What a waste that would be.*

I want to ride on the back of some boy's scooter and feel the wind in my hair. I want to fall deeply in love, even if it hurts. I want to sprawl on Whitney's bed and watch more movies and talk about our dreams of the future, and I want to draw and travel and even learn to dance. And maybe Mom is right about my dad. If he can't accept me, his own flesh and blood, limp and claw and all, maybe he's not worth getting to know.

I curl the fingers of my right hand around the railing and peer into the grotto. I try to conjure the lady in white. Some people said that she was a fairy. Bernadette never actually said that she was the Virgin, but that's what the villagers wanted to believe. I don't see a fairy or anything else. All I see is stone. I heave a sigh of relief and start to walk away.

That's when I hear the voice.

"Forgive," a woman whispers.

My skin goes all prickly. I veer back toward the cave, but there's nothing there. Just stone, as before.

"Forgive," the voice says again, a little louder this time. I turn to see an elderly woman, her eyes squeezed shut. Okay, so she's not talking to me. She's thinking about her own problems. Once again, relief whooshes through me, but this time it's mixed with something else. I think of Mom and all the gifts that she has given me on this trip—the story about my father, the knowledge of my brother, Junpei, this moment at the shrine, even my friendship with Hervé.

I feel a sudden surge of love for my mother. I hurry as fast as I can to find her. When I do, I am as surprised as I've ever been. She's behind all of the rows of chairs, kneeling. Her head is bowed and her hands are folded together. The sight of my mother praying is about as much of a miracle as anything.

"Mom," I say. "Let's go."

She opens her eyes. They are rimmed with red. There are a few streaks on her face. "I'm sorry, Aiko. I'm so sorry about everything."

"It's okay, Mom. I forgive you." I hold out her hand to help her up.

Instead, she opens her palm to me, offering a square of folded paper.

"What's this?" I ask, plucking it from her hand.

"It's your father's address. Do with it what you like."

I hold it for a moment without reading it, and then I put it in my pocket. It's my father's address, but this is also where my brother lives.

31

We hang out in Lourdes for a few more days. We've come all this way, so why not? Mom and I go for a walk around the city, stopping here and there to sketch. It reminds me of old times, when we would sit at the table drawing each other. Today my anger is gone. I don't feel irritated even when Mom puts her hand on my arm to steady me, or guides me through a door.

We find a cool gallery on rue Mozart and stop in to see metal sculptures of dogs, bulls, and birds.

"This artist has a way with the welder, doesn't he?" Mom asks.

"Yeah, sure does." I'm a little relieved to see that Lourdes is about more than the lame and the sick.

There are also horses for riding, and a railway leading to the top of a mountain—Le Pic du Jer—from which we can see the village of Lourdes with all its orange-tiled roofs, Bernadette's old hometown, Pau, and the lush valley below.

Before we leave, we duck into a souvenir shop. It's full of Our Lady of Lourdes key chains and T-shirts. You can buy coasters and silver spoons, and, of course, containers of water. I remember how moved Whitney was by the story of Bernadette and buy a bottle of spring water for her. There's a picture of Bernadette on the label, her hands folded in prayer. The lady in white hovers above her.

The clerk looks at my clawed hand and gives me a sickly sweet smile.

While she's ringing up my purchase, I bite down on my tongue. I want to tell her that the water's not for me, that she doesn't need to feel sorry for me, or hope for a cure, but then again, it's none of her business.

I hand over the money and quickly turn away.

On Friday, we take the train back to Paris.

When we walk into the hotel lobby, I cry out in surprise. "Raoul!"

He's sitting on one of the velvet-upholstered chairs, reading a newspaper.

"Hello, ladies," he says without moving. Is it my imagination, or is he suddenly a little shy?

Mom stops still in her tracks and drops her purse. Incredibly, tears are pooling in her eyes. She picks up her bag, and we go to him together. All three of us stand there hugging and kissing in the hotel lobby.

"I was just reading a review of your show," he says to Mom when we finally break apart.

"I didn't know you could read French," I say.

"*Un petit peu.*" He shrugs. "I could make out some words, like *magnifique* and *radicale.*"

"Are you staying here?" I ask.

"Yeah. I got the art deco room," Raoul says.

"Cool," I say. "Can we see it?"

"Sure. And then I'm taking you both out to dinner."

I slip back into our room to get the CD I bought for Raoul. "This is for you," I say, handing it over.

His face lights up. "Rai! This puts me in the mood for couscous. I bet there's a North African restaurant around here. What do you think?"

"Sounds great," Mom says, linking her arm through his.

I nod in agreement. I've never had couscous, but I trust Raoul. So far everything we've eaten with him has been delicious.

Raoul turns to me and says, "So what's Gadget Girl up to these days?"

My mouth falls open. Did Whitney tell? Did I leave some incriminating evidence in my room? Did he hack my website? "How did you know?"

He shrugs and looks at Mom.

"It's pretty obvious, isn't it?" she says. "All of the evidence is there—the eggbeater, the macchinetta. And there was that story about the giant red sea turtle that crawled into Gadget Girl's camp with a bell on its back. That's a story from the Shikoku Pilgrimage that I told you about. I thought you wanted people to know it was you."

I nod slowly. Maybe she's right. Maybe I did want them to know, underneath it all. And maybe it's time to come out about my work.

"Gadget Girl has gone global," I say, no longer able to contain my enthusiasm. I tell them about Hervé's translation, and about Gadget Girl in chalk on the sidewalks of Paris.

"Good for her," Raoul says with a wink. "Now about that other project."

And then I remember that he's supposed to be babysitting my sprout. I kinda forgot about that when I sent the e-mail inviting him over.

"Oh, yeah. How's my indigo plant doing?"

Raoul's face goes a little cloudy. "I think it misses you. I followed your instructions to the letter, but it started looking a little droopy soon after you left. I even played it some Turkish music, but it didn't seem to do any good. I'm really sorry, Aiko. I know you were counting on me."

Oh, well. I can't exactly blame him for almost killing my plant. And really, what does it matter? I was trying to prove myself as an indigo farmer in order to impress my father. What do I care what he thinks, this man who couldn't open his heart to a tiny, helpless baby, a man who ignores his flesh and blood across the sea? I have nothing to prove to him.

"Don't worry about it," I say to Raoul. "There will be other sprouts."

Mom excuses herself for a moment to ask the concierge for a restaurant recommendation and then leads us out to a cab.

We wind up in a place a few streets away called Le Souk. We're shown to a low table and seated on cushions. Arabian dance music pulses from the speakers in the corner, and the scent of mint and cooking meat fills the air. A waiter wearing a red fez brings us menus and sprinkles water on our hands.

Raoul brings his fingers to his nose. "Orange blossom water," he tells us. He peruses the menu, then orders a tagine.

"You'll like it," he says. "It's meat and dried fruit cooked in a special clay pot."

While we wait for our food, Mom fills Raoul in on our sightseeing activities. She glosses over our trip to Lourdes, and doesn't mention Hervé at all. That's for me to tell.

The waiter brings a pot of mint tea and pours us each a cup.

Raoul raises his. "A toast," he says, "in honor of Aiko's fifteenth birthday."

"It's already over," I say, embarrassed.

"Nevertheless."

We clink cups, and then he pulls a small package from his jacket pocket. "Happy birthday."

I open it slowly, trying to prepare my reaction. I remember all the awful gifts I got from Mom's previous boyfriend, the effort that it took to appear glad. They are both watching me, which makes it all worse.

But when I've unwrapped the small box and opened the lid, I gasp. Inside is a dozen pairs of high heels—charms dangling from a bracelet. These are the high-heeled shoes presented to girls at their quinceañeras. "Thank you! It's perfect!"

"May I?" Raoul reaches across the table.

I hand over the bracelet, and he clasps it around my wrist.

"And now," he says, reaching into his other pocket and pulling out another small fuzzy box, "would you have me as your stepfather?"

I look across the table at Mom. Her eyes are filled with tears—happy tears, judging by the smile trembling on her lips. She sees the question in my eyes and nods.

"Yes," I say. "I would."

He opens the box. The diamond glitters in the lamplight. We all admire it for a moment, there against the blue velvet, before he removes it and slides it onto my mother's ring finger. They kiss.

I smile, tears pooling in my eyes as well. "I think this calls for champagne."

We are almost too happy to eat, but then the food comes, and it's irresistible. The waiter brings a clay pot with a cone-shaped lid. The lid is lifted, releasing a rich, spicy aroma, and we ladle lamb stewed with pears, almonds, and raisins onto beds of couscous.

When the champagne arrives, I am allowed a sip. It's not enough to make me drunk, but I feel giddy— giddy enough so that when the other patrons start grooving to the techno-Arabian music, I don't even resist when Raoul pulls me to my feet. There, in Le Souk, I get my first dance.

32

"Raoul and I are going to do some sightseeing. Do you want to come?"

I've already seen the Eiffel Tower and Sacré-Cœur, and I think the two of them could use some time alone, so I pass. "I'm feeling inspired," I say. "I want to work on my manga."

Mom nods. There is no argument. She understands the heart of an artist.

At first I think I'll work in the hotel room. But I'd really rather be downstairs in the café. Maybe someday *Gadget Girl* will take off and visitors will flock to see my favorite table. I imagine my spot being cordoned off, like the booth at the place in London where J.K. Rowling drank coffee and wrote stories about Harry Potter. If all goes well, I could put Hervé's family business on the map.

I pack up my drawing materials and notebook and head to the cafe.

Hervé's father greets me with a big smile.

"*Un citron pressé,*" I say, ordering a drink made from citrus fruit. It's time to try something different.

"*Tout de suite,*" he promises, and goes off to get my beverage.

Hervé's not there. Which is maybe just as well. I've got work to do.

Over the past couple of weeks, I've been thinking about giving up on *Gadget Girl* altogether. But that wouldn't be fair to my loyal fans—Brandy in Alaska! Zack in Tallahassee!—and I think I need to tie up the story. Or at least take it to the next level. And I want everyone to know, finally, that I'm the one who created the comic.

This next episode will be called *Gadget Girl Falls in Love.* Maybe a little too sappy for Chad and Luke, but who cares? In this edition, Gadget Girl will meet the Kitchen Musician. He'll be a Latino who's also good with his hands—part Robert Johnson, part Anthony Bourdain, a guy who can charm with his guitar playing *and* his cooking. The Kitchen Musician will not be a dude-in-distress—not even close. He'll join forces with Gadget Girl. They'll be partners. And Chaz Whittaker? I guess he'll just have to fend for himself.

I look out the window. I see *la parfumerie* across the street, a mocha-colored woman in high heels and a flowing scarf walking her dog, a glimpse of a gargoyle. Of course this story will be set in Paris.

It'll all be there—a daring rescue from the top of the Eiffel Tower, a romantic cruise along the Seine, numerous cups of strong coffee and hot chocolate at sidewalk cafés. As soon as I open my notebook, my pencil starts flying across the page. Right now I'm just making rough sketches, getting the ideas down. The refinement comes later.

I've already decided that this will be my wedding gift for Mom and Raoul. They're talking about getting married in a couple of months, so I don't have a lot of time.

I'm so intent on my drawing that it takes me a moment to notice that someone is standing next to me.

"Can I join you?"

I look up, startled to see Hervé, standing there. He's wearing jeans and a tight grey T-shirt. Obviously it's his day off.

"Have a seat," I say, trying to keep my voice cool.

"Where have you been?" Hervé leans forward across the table. "I saw you walk by the café the other day and you didn't come in. And then—*pouf!*—you disappeared."

The knot in my stomach begins to unravel. I'm suddenly not so sure about what I saw. "You were talking to that girl…"

He frowns. "You mean Celeste?"

"Yes," I say. "Why didn't you tell me you had a girlfriend?"

He shakes his head. "She is not my girlfriend. Not anymore. We break up, we get back together, we break up again. It makes me crazy." He fills his cheeks with air, then implodes them. "Enough! I told her that we are finished for good this time."

I don't know what to say, so I state the obvious. "You don't have to work today."

He reaches across the table and takes my hand. "No. So maybe I will just sit here with you?"

I smile and nod. Although I remind myself that there is really nothing between us, I can't help but feel happy. Just being here together is enough for now. In a few years our age difference won't be such a big deal. And then? Who knows.

"What are you drawing?" he asks.

"It's really rough," I say, "but, here." I pull my hand gently away from his and push the sketchbook toward him. I tell him about Raoul's arrival and my mother's engagement. And then I outline the basics of the story I've come up with.

"Nice," he says. "I hope you will send me a copy when it's finished."

"Yeah, of course." This seems like the perfect time to exchange contact info, so I write down my e-mail and Facebook addresses and hand them over to Hervé. He does the same. Suddenly, France doesn't seem all that far away from Michigan.

"Will you come to the airport to see me off?" I ask. "I mean, I would like you to."

"*Bien sur.*"

PART SIX

michigan, again

"There is no place like home."

—Dorothy

33

As we ride in the cab to the airport, I watch out the window, trying to memorize everything about this city. I take in the grey stone buildings, the chic thin women, the yappy little dogs on leashes. I look out the back window at the Eiffel Tower receding in the distance. I say good-bye to the City of Lights, the capital of fashion. The City of Love.

There is an entourage waiting at the airport to see us off—Giselle, Monsieur Le Clerc, all of the gallery workers, Etienne and his wife, and, best of all, Hervé.

When he comes over to me, he seems a little bit shy. I think he might even be the tiniest bit sad. He leads me away from the others, till we're standing in front of a white pillar.

"So I guess this is *adieu*," I say, thinking to impress him with my French.

He frowns. "Not *adieu*. That means good-bye forever. I hope to see you again."

His words make me feel like leaping, like singing

and dancing. Like doing cartwheels and jumping jacks. "Me too," I say. "Maybe you could visit America again."

A fantasy springs to mind: Hervé, as an exchange student at my new high school. Madison Fox looking on in jealousy as we walk down the hallway holding hands. The two of us all dressed up for an autograph party for my newly published manga at the local Kinko's, er, bookstore.

"Or maybe we will meet in Japan someday?" he says.

Another fantasy: Hervé and me, at the top of Tokyo Sky Tree, looking down at the metropolis below, or sipping green tea lattes in the Gundam robot cafe, or even the two of us swimming with the loggerhead turtles off the coast of Shikoku.

"That would be cool," I say.

And then something incredible happens. Hervé puts his finger on my chin and tips my face up. Then he ducks down and kisses me. Softly, gently. When his lips brush against mine, my whole body feels warm and bright. It's as if my skin is sparkling. *This is what it's like to swallow a star.*

Mom, Raoul, and about a million other people are watching, but I hardly notice them. When Hervé steps back, I'm breathless.

"*Au revoir,*" he says softly. "That means, 'until the next time.'"

"*Au revoir,*" I reply.

We stand there together until after the call for small children and passengers needing assistance, until almost everyone else has boarded the plane, and then I make my way to the gate, my eyes on him until I have to turn to go down the skywalk. And then I'm on the plane, on my way back to the U.S.

For the first hour or so, I'm too distracted to read or sketch or do much of anything. I replay that kiss over and over, and then I revisit every moment I spent with Hervé, starting with that first cup of hot chocolate.

Finally, the flight attendant comes down the aisle, pushing her meal cart. "Beef or chicken?" she asks. She has a French accent.

"Chicken," Mom says absentmindedly.

I glance over at her sketchpad. She's been drawing a girl, or maybe it's a woman. She's standing in a cave, hands reaching out, eyes gazing toward heaven. I suddenly realize that she's sketching Bernadette Soubirous. Hmm. Could she be entering a new phase?

When the flight attendant looks at me, I look up at her and smile. *"Le boeuf, s'il vous plaît."*

The flight from Paris to Detroit is nine hours, after which we change planes and hop a commuter to Grand Rapids. From there it's a forty-five minute drive to our home near Lake Michigan. By the time we arrive on our doorstep, night has fallen. It's too late to drop by Whitney's house, but as soon as our suitcases are brought inside, I go to my computer and log in to send her a message: "When can we meet?"

She must be online, because she replies right away. "Tomorrow. How about 11AM? How was Paris???"

"Later," I reply. I've got so much to tell her, but I want to do it in person. This is life-changing stuff. If we're laughing and crying together, we should be in the same room, close enough to hug. I brush my teeth and put on my pajamas. Mom and Raoul are still in the living room, decompressing from our trip. They're sitting on the sofa with glasses of wine. Somehow I don't think Raoul will be going back to his apartment tonight.

"Good night," I say. I go over and give each of them a kiss.

"Sleep well." Mom runs her palm over my head.

"Good night, Aiko. Sweet dreams," Raoul says.

I'm exhausted, but I can't get to sleep. A million things are going through my head. What will Whitney have to say about Hervé? Will Hervé send an e-mail soon? Should I write to my brother? And what should I call Raoul after the wedding? Dad? Papa? Raoul? My body is on Paris time. It's telling me that I should be waking up for hot chocolate and croissants right about now, not tunneling under a duvet. I toss and turn for another hour or so before I finally fall asleep.

I wake up way too early—jet lag again. The rest

of the house is quiet. Mom is still asleep. I check my
e-mail. Nothing yet. I get out my sketchbook and spend
an hour or so working on *Gadget Girl Falls in Love.*

When I hear clattering in the kitchen, I venture
out of my room to find Raoul at the stove. The aroma
of freshly brewed coffee fills the air.

"How does a Spanish omelet sound?" he asks.

"Sounds great." I don't think I've ever had one
before, but I'm sure it'll be delicious.

I read the newspaper while he grates and beats and
fries.

By the time Mom gets up, breakfast is laid out on
the table. As it turns out, a Spanish omelet is made
with onions and potatoes, sliced thin and fried till
they're sort of chewy in the middle. It's the best
omelet I've ever tasted.

After breakfast I help to load the dishwasher and
then get ready to go to Whitney's house. Mom drops
me off about an hour later.

Whitney's mother answers the door. It's a weekday
and, unlike the rest of us, she has to work. (Mom and
Raoul's classes don't start up for another two weeks.)
She's decked out in a summer-weight suit, her face all
made up. No sweatpants today.

I find Whitney in bed with a black-and-white
movie playing. She's wearing a faded University of
Michigan T-shirt and a pair of leggings, and there's a
pile of celebrity gossip magazines on her nightstand.

"Aiko!" She opens her arms to me, and I flop down beside her. "So how was Paris? Tell me!"

"First tell me about you. How was camping?"

"Pfft. You don't want to know. I got into some poison oak or something and got this hideous rash." She pulls up her leggings and shows me her calf, all mottled red.

"Oh, well, maybe I can help you out," I said. "I got you some water from the spring at Lourdes."

She raises her eyebrows. "You went to Lourdes?"

"Yeah," I say. "I was in such a rush to get over here that I forgot to dig the bottle out of my suitcase. I'll bring it next time, okay? I did remember to grab this, though." I reach into my bag and take out a scarf and a pair of earrings that I bought for Whitney at an open air market in Paris. "Here."

Whitney unfurls the scarf, which is dyed in the bright colors of a Matisse painting, and holds it in front of her eyes. "I love it. Thank you."

I try to get her to share more about her vacation, so she tells me about the raccoons that raided their campsite, and the two days of rain that soaked through their tent and finally drove them to a motel down the road.

"Have you heard from Luke?"

"Yeah." She blushes. "As a matter of fact, we're going to go see a movie together this Friday." She looks at me nervously. Until now, she and I have always gone to see movies together. There was never any boy in the way, no one to compete for my attention. And vice versa.

"I met this really cute guy in Paris," I tell her.

I can see that she's immediately relieved. "Tell me, tell me!" She bounces on the bed.

"His name is Hervé." I tell her about everything—his giraffe eyes and curling sideburns, riding on the back of his scooter, our night at Le Moulin Rouge, how I fell and the way that he caught me. Of course I tell her about the gallery opening, and the French celebrities surrounding *Aiko, En Pointe*, and Celeste, and the kiss at the airport. And then I tell her about my brother, and the fact that my father knows about me, and how he didn't want me because of my disability. I start crying and Whitney reaches out her hand for mine.

I sob as I've never sobbed before. I throw myself down next to Whitney, and even though I know I'm getting snot and tears on her comforter, she doesn't say a word. She just holds my hand and strokes my hair until I'm all cried out. And then she hands me a box of tissues.

"I bet if he met you now, he'd think you were awesome," she says.

Now that I have his address, I guess I can decide if I'll meet him again or not. But it's not something I want to think about right now.

"My dad didn't want me either," Whitney says quietly. "He didn't fight Mom for custody. He didn't even ask if he could take Nathan and me with him. He just left, and now he has a new family."

Well, we'll still have that in common, even if she starts going to movies and dances with someone else and sits at a different lunch table.

And then it's as if she's reading my mind. "You know, nothing is going to change."

"Yeah," I say, but things are changing already. There's Luke, for one thing. And we'll be starting high school in a couple of weeks—new kids, new classes, new teachers. There's no way that things can stay the same, but I know that we will always be friends. For now and the foreseeable future, Whitney is the one I'll tell my secrets to.

"Oh, I almost forgot to tell you," I say. "I've decided to put my name on the next issue of *Gadget Girl*."

Whitney nods, as if I've made a wise choice. "People should know how amazingly talented you are," she says.

And then I tell her about the upcoming wedding and my soon-to-be-stepdad, which, of course, makes her squeal.

"So what happened at Lourdes?" she asks, when I think I've finally run out of things to say.

"Oh, yeah. Lourdes." I tell her about the pilgrims and the grotto and the woman who said "forgive."

And how I realized right then that I didn't even want to be different from who I am.

Whitney is quiet for a long moment. Then she says, "Maybe that woman wasn't talking about you and your mom. Maybe she meant that you should forgive your *father.*"

34

That afternoon, Raoul goes to his apartment and brings back my indigo plant.

"I'm sorry," he says, although he's already apologized and I've already forgiven him.

He hands over the little pot. The seedling that I had imagined would be lush and leafy right about now is a shriveled sprout. Any other person would give up at this point and start over, but I still have hope. I put it back in its usual place, at the edge of my desk in a circle of lamplight, knowing that it's going to take more than just a few beams to cure this baby. And then I have an idea.

The bottle of holy water that I bought for Whitney is still sitting on my dresser. I grab it and study the label for a few minutes. This is the water that cured the Emperor's baby and the bullet-riddled solider. At any rate, this water isn't going to hurt my plant.

I screw off the top and tip the bottle over the withering seedling just enough so that a few drops wet the soil. I sprinkle another couple of drops on the tiny, curled-up leaves, and screw the top back on.

Japanese is way more complicated than French or Spanish. For starters, there are three different writing systems—hiragana, which is a phonetic alphabet consisting of 47 letters; katakana, which is a simplified version of hiragana and is used for words borrowed from foreign languages, like "cheeseburger"; and kanji, those ideograms from China that look like trees and picnic tables. And then there are different vocabularies depending on whether you're male or female, younger or older, royal or not. So far, using workbooks and a few key websites, I've mastered hiragana, katakana, and a few kanji, which enabled me to write the following letter last night:

"To Junpei,

Today is sunny. [Note: In Japan, you're supposed to start out talking about the weather.]

I am Aiko. I am your sister. I am fifteen years old. You are my brother. I am happy. I like manga. Do you like manga?

From Aiko.

It's a poor excuse for a letter, I know, but it's the best I can do in my self-taught baby Japanese.

Art can be understood in any language. A picture is worth a thousand words and all that. I tuck a couple of issues of *Gadget Girl* into a manila envelope. I also include last year's school portrait and a leaf plucked from my indigo plant. I figure he's spent some time in the fields, so he should be able to identify it. And then I dig a bunch of stamps out of Mom's desk drawer and mail it to my half brother in Japan.

On the first day of school, I wake to find that my indigo plant has definitely perked up. It has grown— count them—two inches, and greened up nicely. A miracle, I would say, and an excellent beginning to ninth grade.

In celebration, I decide to wear my Frida skirt—the white one with the folkloric appliquéd flowers. Mom is allowing me to wear mascara. She even helps me put it on. Raoul makes a special breakfast—blueberry pancakes with maple syrup—and offers to drive me to school in his convertible. I bundle up hot-off-the-press copies of *Gadget Girl Falls in Love*, and put them in my backpack. I'm thinking this issue is my best work yet.

Whitney meets me at the school entrance. She's wearing a T-shirt and a crinkly gauze skirt.

We have English together, first period, but class doesn't start for another fifteen minutes, so we station ourselves against the lockers in the hallway. I hand over a pile of comics to Whitney. We pass them out to anyone coming through who shows the slightest bit of interest.

Luke spots us from thirty feet away. He's grown over the summer, and his brown hair is now streaked with blond. He must have spent some time at the beach. "Yo, ladies!" he says, coming closer. "Whatcha got there?"

"The new issue of *Gadget Girl*!" Whitney says.

Luke lights up. "Gimme, gimme!" He practically rips one out of Whitney's hand and flips to the first page. He has yet to notice that I've included my byline on the cover.

I foist a copy upon Jason Tran, who looks up in surprise after he sees my name, and pass out a few to the cheerleaders. I'm down to my last copy when the bell rings, signaling first period. Whitney has successfully unloaded all of hers.

"Well, it's done!" she says, slightly breathless from exhilaration. "We've outed you as author."

"Yeah." I think of the handful of harsh reviews my mother has suffered. Not everyone gets or appreciates her work, but that's the way it is with art. There may be some people who don't like *Gadget Girl* and who will be more than willing to tell me about it. There may be some people who make a big deal of my disability—"Look! The crip girl can actually do something!" When you put yourself out there in art or in love—or in life in general—you're risking rejection. I think I can handle it, though. Or at least I'm willing to give it a try.

Whitney and I make our way to English. The class-room is full of familiar faces, and a few new ones. I see that Chad Renquist has already staked out a seat in the back row. There are a couple of empty desks up at the front. "Can you save me a seat?" I ask Whitney.

"Sure," she says.

I take a deep breath and walk up to Chad. My heart is banging against my rib cage. I concentrate on every step, to make sure I don't fall. "Here," I say, holding out the comic book to him. "I heard you were a fan."

I wait for him and his friends to say something mean about my leg or my mom or my art, but they don't. Maybe they went through some changes over the summer, too.

"Thanks," Chad says. He accepts my small gift and looks at the cover. I turn to go to my desk.

"Aiko," Chad says.

"Yeah?" It's been years since he's said my name. I turn around, and he is looking straight at me.

"Your work is really good."

I smile. "Thanks." And then I remember all of his assignments in middle school art class. Blue Chad. A painting he did of the lighthouse. "Yours, too."

35

The day before my mother's wedding, I open my e-mail to find a reply from Junpei. It's short, but sweet. He wants to set up a meeting via webcam for the following Saturday morning at eleven, eastern standard time. In one week, I will get to chat with my long-lost half brother face to face! But what if he doesn't speak English? I'll have to practice some Japanese phrases. I'll have to prepare some pictures. I need to choose an outfit. Suddenly, there is so much going on all at once. I can only concentrate on one thing at a time.

So. The wedding.

If it were me, ten or fifteen years in the future, getting married to, say, Hervé, or some grown-up version of Chad, I'd chuck every black thing in my closet and wear a huge, poufy white gown. So what if it had a train that could trip me up? My groom would be there to catch me. Best-case scenario, a wedding is a once-in-a-lifetime event, so I'd want it to be a big deal.

Mom and Raoul's ceremony, however, is surprisingly

low-key, considering it's the first time for both of them. We're having it in our backyard, with the lilac bushes and the bird feeder. Only a small group has gathered. Mom's family is represented by my grandparents, of course. Raoul's mother is here, as well as his sister and her kids. Whitney, her mom, and Nathan have come over, along with some of Mom's and Raoul's friends and colleagues from work. They've hired a female judge to officiate. Through Mom's bedroom window, I can see the guests milling about.

Mom steps into a simple burgundy sheath, the color of the maples at the edge of our yard.

"You would have looked great in a white gown," I say. "You know, like Princess Diana wore? Or something by Vera Wang."

Mom stands with her back to me, waiting to be zipped up. "Princess Di was only twenty-one when she got married. I'm too old for that. Besides, I can wear this dress again."

I close up her dress with one hand, and she turns around, bringing us face to face. She holds me by the shoulders firmly, bracing me. "Are you ready for this?"

I nod. My arm starts to spaz a little. I feel kind of nervous, but I'm sure she does, too. I've never had a dad before, and she's never had a husband. It'll take some getting used to.

"Okay, one, two, three," she says, and we both take

a deep breath. And exhale. We hold hands as we go out of the bedroom, through the living room, and out the back door. We walk into music—a Mexican wedding song wafting from stereo speakers—and over the soft grass, to where Raoul stands waiting. He's dressed in a suit, not a tux, and he's smiling at both of us.

I stand next to them as they exchange vows. When Mom says "I do," my body goes still. Calm.

Raoul says, "I will," and I feel as if I've been covered in a blanket of safety and love. Before there were just two of us, and now there are three.

The judge, in her navy suit, tells them that they can kiss. As their lips come together, everyone starts to clap. When they break apart and turn toward the gathering, the guests toss birdseed at them. It rains down on Mom's hair and dress, making her laugh.

"Okay," Raoul says. "Let the party begin!"

I move toward the card table where the wedding cake is, but I know that Raoul doesn't mean just now. He's talking about the rest of our lives.

36

Mom and Raoul don't go on a honeymoon trip. We've just been to France, and the school year has already begun, so we spend the next week settling in, getting used to each other, and finding space for Raoul's stuff.

All of this helps the week go by quickly, bringing me to Saturday morning and my first meeting with my half brother.

I show up in front of the computer thirty minutes early. I boot up, check into Skype and arrange my Japanese cheat sheet. I check the number of hits to my website—twenty more since yesterday—and my e-mail inbox. I wait for my brother to call.

And then Junpei is up on my screen. His hair is super short, like an army recruit's, and he's wearing glasses with heavy black rims. I can see a shelf lined with books in the background. A pennant from some baseball team.

"Konnichiwa!" I say. I've got my greetings down pat.

He looks a little confused. Was my pronunciation that bad? Or was he just surprised to hear me speaking Japanese?

After a few seconds, he replies. *"Konbanwa."* Good evening.

Oh, right. I forgot about the time difference. It's already evening on the other side of the globe.

"Watashi wa Aiko desu," I say, forging on. Duh. Like he doesn't already know who I am. Who else would be at this number? But I've about exhausted my conversational Japanese.

"My name is Junpei."

"Watashi wa ju go sai." I tell him my age.

"I'm thirteen years old," he replies.

"Watashi wa manga ga suki desu." I tell him that I like manga.

"I like manga, too," he says. "And baseball."

Apparently, that's about all he can manage in English, because we're both silent after that. We seem unable to do anything but grin at each other like a couple of fools.

Finally, he holds up his hand and says, *"Chotto matte."* His body unbends and he disappears from the screen. To go get his dictionary? Or something to draw with?

But then I hear muffled voices, and a new face appears. A kind, sad face with wrinkles raying out from the corners of his eyes. A wide forehead like mine. Eyebrows, short and fat, like a couple of cater-pillars stuck on his forehead. My father's face.

"Hello," he says.

A lump forms in my throat. For a moment, I can't say anything at all in any language.

I feel like Dorothy, meeting the Wizard of Oz at last, and finding out that he's just an ordinary guy. He doesn't look evil, or like a hero. He looks normal. Hopeful. Like someone who messed up and wants to do better the next time.

"Hello?" he says again. "Can you hear me?"

I take a deep breath. "Y-yes. I'm here. I'm Aiko."

He nods. "I know." And then it's as if he's the one with the lump in his throat. He swallows hard, brushes a hand over his eyes, and says, "My daughter." His voice breaks, and I almost wish I could reach into the computer screen and pat him on the shoulder. I feel kind of sorry for him.

There are so many things that I want to say—too many—but for now, all I can do is stare. With his head bent toward his chest, I can see that his hair is thinning on top. His shoulders are a little slumped. I wonder what about him attracted my mother back in the day, in Paris. I wait for him to collect himself. When he does, he holds up a leaf.

"Where did you get this?" he asks.

It's the indigo leaf that I'd sent to Junpei, and it's looking a little tattered after that transoceanic flight. "I grew it myself," I say. A burst of pride shoots through me. "I wanted to learn to be an indigo farmer."

He smiles. "Maybe you'd like to come and see our farm."

Yes, I would, or I thought that I would. I don't know any more. My feelings are in flux. I understand that this is an invitation, but I haven't quite forgiven him yet. And my heart is still back in France, with Hervé. I wouldn't mind going back to Paris. "Maybe," I say.

"My wife would welcome you," he continues. "She has always wanted a daughter."

And my grandparents? I wonder, but I can't bring myself to ask. Does he want me to go live with him, then? Does he think that I would abandon Mom, just like that? After all we've been through?

"Maybe next summer," I say. "I could go for a visit." That gives me nine months to get into the right frame of mind.

He nods. "I will be waiting for you."

After a moment, he bows and moves away from the camera. Junpei reappears. He holds up a manga— *Black Jack*, one of my favorites.

"I love that," I say, nodding. I grab some of my own manga to show him.

We take turns sharing, nodding and smiling, and finally I hold up the first page of my new story, *Indigo Girl*.

He gives me the thumbs-up sign.

I silently vow to work harder on my Japanese, and we sign off.

When the screen goes blank, I sit there for a long time, frozen, trying to absorb what just happened. A few months ago, I would have been thrilled to connect with my father, to be invited to Japan. I would have had my suitcase packed by the end of our conversation. Now I'm not quite sure how I feel. But he is my father. And I can tell that he's sorry. I should give him a chance. And Junpei is my brother. As the knowledge seeps in, I begin to thaw. A seed breaks open and something begins to grow. Something like possibility.

"*Otosan*," I whisper. *Father*.

I hear voices calling me from somewhere else in the house. I pull out of my deep thoughts and go into the kitchen, where lunch is laid out on the table, to join Mom and Raoul, my ever-growing family.

acknowledgments

Thanks to all who have read and commented upon this story at various stages including Caron K, Margaret Stawowy, Andy Couturier, Helene Dunbar, Holly Thompson, Katrina Grigg-Saito, Leza Lowitz, Alvina Ling, Micol Ostow, Raquel Cool, and Amy Lin. Thank you, Tracy Slater, for the chance to read a portion at Four Stories, Osaka; Debby Vetter and all the fine folks at *Cicada* for publishing a section in somewhat different form as the story "Pilgrimage"; SCBWI for recognizing that story with a Magazine Merit Award; SCBWI-Tokyo for ongoing support and encouragement; and YALITCHAT for more of the same. And finally, I am so grateful to Trish O'Hare for publishing this book.

about the author

Suzanne Kamata was born and raised in Grand Haven, Michigan, where she started her career writing for her high school newspaper. She studied English and French in college and spent several months of foreign study in Avignon. After graduation, she moved to Japan on the JET Program to teach English and has lived there ever since. Suzanne, her husband, and their twins live on the island of Aizumi, a town famous for its indigo.

Suzanne is the author of four books of fiction including the novel, *Losing Kei,* and a short story collection, *The Beautiful One Has Come*, which won a Silver Nautilus Award and was long-listed for the Frank O'Connor International Short Story Award. She has edited three anthologies, among them *Love You to Pieces: Creative Writers on Raising a Child with Special Needs.* Her short stories for young adults and children have appeared in publications such as *Ladybug, Skipping Stones, Cicada, Sucker Literary Magazine* and *Tomo: Friendship Through Fiction—An Anthology of Japan Teen Stories.*

"Pilgrimage," the novella that inspired *Gadget Girl*, was originally published in Cicada. It won the SCBWI Magazine Merit Award for Fiction and was later published in an anthology of the best stories from Cicada's first ten years.

Paris is one of Suzanne's favorite places to visit.

CPSIA information can be obtained at www.ICGtesting.com
Printed in the USA
BVOW071639050513

319883BV00001B/1/P